'There will b

The interruption m...
stand.'

'Then let me spell ... ...ky smile was somehow infinitely more alarming than his raging anger had been. Now he was in control. A shiver of apprehension traced its way down Erin's spine. 'No separation, no divorce—not now, not ever!'

'What do you mean?' she asked in a small voice, even though his statement had been clear enough. This was her worst nightmare coming true.

'You wish me to spell it out again…? My child will not be brought up not knowing his father, his family, not speaking his own language. You will come back to Italy with me, where our child will be born.'

Erin tried to laugh, but all that emerged was a high-pitched squeaky sound. 'You can't force me…' The reminder was as much for her own benefit as his.

His jaw tightened. 'Perhaps you need reminding why you married me in the first instance?'

Her head came up with a jerk. As their eyes clashed there was a tension in the air that reminded Erin of the heavy heat that preceded a storm.

'Come to bed with me.'

Kim Lawrence lives on a farm in rural Anglesey. She runs two miles daily, and finds this an excellent opportunity to unwind and seek inspiration for her writing! It also helps her keep up with her husband, two active sons, and the various stray animals which have adopted them. Always a fanatical consumer of fiction, she is now equally enthusiastic about writing. She loves a happy ending!

Recent titles by the same author:

THE SPANIARD'S PREGNANCY PROPOSAL
THE ITALIAN'S WEDDING ULTIMATUM
THE CARIDES PREGNANCY
SANTIAGO'S LOVE-CHILD

CLAIMING HIS PREGNANT WIFE

BY
KIM LAWRENCE

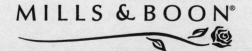

MILLS & BOON®

First published in Great Britain 2007
Harlequin Mills & Boon Limited,
Eton House, 18-24 Paradise Road, Richmond, Surrey TW9 1SR

© Kim Lawrence 2007

ISBN-13: 978 0 263 85334 6

Set in Times Roman 10½ on 12¾ pt
01-0707-48082

Printed and bound in Spain
by Litografia Rosés, S.A., Barcelona

CLAIMING HIS PREGNANT WIFE

CHAPTER ONE

FRANCESCO ROMANELLI had pulled into the outside lane of the motorway when the mobile phone in his pocket began to vibrate again. An impatient grimace furrowing the smooth olive-toned skin of his high, intelligent forehead, he studiously ignored it. However, the interruption did cause his attention to briefly stray to the empty passenger seat where another phone lay, this one switched off.

It was about the only thing that had survived his blitz, when he had gone through the home they had briefly shared and removed every item that had even remotely reminded him of his broken marriage and his wife. Or so he had thought.

If his diligent housekeeper hadn't been so thorough in her war against dust he would have remained ignorant of the phone's existence, and, more importantly, ignorant of its explosive contents.

Which was presumably just what his wife had intended.

What else was he meant to think?

Francesco's jaw clenched as he fought to contain the sense of molten outrage that threatened to overwhelm him every time he thought of the situation he now faced. In fact, he had thought of little else for the past four days and was now digging pretty deep into his reserves of self-restraint!

After the events of the previous months it seemed darkly ironic, he reflected, releasing a self-derisive grunt, that this time last year he had been complaining to his twin brother that his life had become too predictable!

At the time Francesco had just split from his current lover. It had been a civilised parting of the ways, much as their arrangement had been. Normally considered pretty perceptive, Francesco hadn't seen it coming. However, with the wisdom of hindsight he realised that the writing had been on the wall when she had asked him where he thought their relationship was going.

Francesco had been forced to admit that he did not see it going anywhere specifically.

It had not crossed his mind at the time that she would have any problem with his admission. Why would it? The lady in question, a corporate lawyer who was as smart as she was beautiful, had gone out of her way at the outset of their relationship to warn him that she had no time in her life for emotional entanglements. So it had come as some surprise to Francesco to hear her say, 'Nothing personal, Francesco, I've actually never had better sex, but with my body clock ticking I can't afford to waste my time with a man—even one as lovely as you—who is commitment-phobic.'

Francesco had not been offended by her comments or lost any sleep over them, but they had made him wonder...'Do you think I'm commitment-phobic?' he later asked his twin.

Rafe's response was tactful. 'Of course not, but maybe if you put as much effort into your personal relationships as you do work?'

'That's the problem. I *don't* have to put that much effort into work...some days,' he admitted. 'I find myself hoping that there will be a disaster just so that I can fix it...there's just no buzz. My life is totally predictable. There are no real challenges—nothing to get the adrenaline pumping.'

'Maybe there's a life-changing surprise around the corner, Francesco,' his brother suggested, looking amused.

'*Dio mio*, I hope so.'

What did they say? You should be careful what you wish for because it might come true!

Maybe, Francesco speculated darkly, life-changing scenarios were like buses—after a long drought when they did come they came thick and fast!

And they rarely took the guise you anticipated.

In his case in the space of a few months he had suffered the devastating loss of his twin brother in tragic circumstances and, while still coming to terms with that loss, had discovered love at first sight was not merely confined to the pages of romantic fiction.

Though maybe marrying the person you fell in love with within five days should be!

As Francesco looked down at the brown finger on his left hand that was encircled by the heavy gold band his grip tightened on the steering wheel. His upper lip curled contemptuously: *love!* It hadn't been love, he told himself grimly. It had been a combination of lust and blind infatuation.

Some people might have suggested that his reaction to the letter that had arrived a week earlier from Erin suggested something more than infatuation or lust. But they didn't understand the extent of his problem with failure, and wasn't that essentially what divorce was?

Admittedly, walking out of the office two minutes before an important meeting without telling anyone where he was going, getting onto a plane and heading for England with the intention of explaining to his wife in person that he would *never* give her her freedom was a pretty strong reaction to the suggestion of failure.

But he would have explained to these doubters that failure was a word that had never been in his vocabulary. Failure was something that happened to other people. His premise in life had always been that if you wanted something badly enough you made it happen, you fought for what you wanted.

The plane had been landing when the thought had hit him. Why should he even try and fight for her? He didn't want her.

What would I want with a woman who doesn't trust me?

Francesco knew that Erin might even construe his arrival as the first move to reconciling their relationship, and that just wasn't going to happen. She was the one in the wrong.

The one he had expected to come crawling back.

His gaze shifted back to the empty passenger seat. When the phone had surfaced the information it contained had changed everything.

Who made the *first move* was suddenly no longer important. There was no decision to make; divorce was quite simply no longer an option. If Erin had been halfway adult she would have realised this, too.

The situation required immediate action. Cool, clear-headed action.

Francesco's dark glance slewed once more towards the phone…a muscle along the angle of his jaw clenched as he wrenched his straying attention back onto the road ahead. At this moment he felt neither cool nor clear-headed.

But he did feel grimly determined.

It was sobering to acknowledge how close he had been to throwing the phone away. Fortunately something had made him switch it on before he had done so.

Erin had one message.

His steelily determined eyes fixed on the road ahead, Francesco recalled the moment when he had heard the polite voice on the machine apologise, and explain that the date of Mrs Romanelli's next antenatal appointment had been brought forward a week.

His normally sharp, analytic mind numb, he had replayed the message three times before it had finally clicked.

He was going to be a father!

A man was meant to feel elation and joy at such a moment, but Erin had robbed him of that. Just as it now appeared increasingly likely she had planned to rob him of his child. He wondered how he would ever be able to forgive her for that.

Had she ever been going to tell him?

Even though over the last few days he had analysed the situation from every angle countless times, weighing up the possible explanations for her silence, no matter how hard he tried he still couldn't come up with any halfway adequate excuse.

He had even given her the benefit of the doubt and accepted that she might not have known that she was pregnant when she had left, but she must have known for weeks now.

Weeks during which she hadn't made any attempt to contact him except with that one letter expressing her wish to divorce as soon as possible. Erin had made a definite choice *not* to tell him he was going to be a father. The knowledge stuck in his throat like bitter bile.

She had taken a unilateral decision as though he were irrelevant. Even if she had decided they had no future together there were things to discuss…arrangements…options! Not that there was more than one option as far as he was concerned. Francesco was firmly of the belief that there was only one way to bring up a child, especially his, and that was with two parents.

And it wasn't as if she had had to contact him. He had tried to contact her and given her every opportunity to tell him, but had simply been given the runaround, fobbed off by her wretched, manipulative mother.

Did Erin really imagine for one moment that she could have his baby without him finding out? The hard laugh that was drawn from his throat was cut off as the phone in his pocket began to ring again—whoever was trying to contact him was not giving up—and with a sigh of irritation he indicated to leave the motorway.

Erin had been surprised when Francesco's cousin Valentina had contacted her and invited her to spend the weekend at the country home where she and her English husband Sam ran a stud farm.

It crossed her mind that Valentina did not know that she and Francesco had split up. She didn't want anyone running away with the idea she felt as though her heart had been ripped out and in her most casual tone she had asked, 'You do know that Francesco and I…that we're not together?'

'Yes, I know, and I'm really sorry,' replied the Italian woman. 'But it doesn't mean we can't still be friends, does it?'

Erin had been reluctant to accept the invitation, but Valentina had been so enthusiastic about seeing her that in the end Erin had felt it would be churlish to throw her kindness back in her face.

Erin had arrived the previous evening and Valentina had explained that the other weekend guests were not expected until today. She glanced at her watch and wondered if anyone had arrived yet.

It was the distinctive sound of horse hooves that drew Erin to the window of the sunny sitting room. Outside in the courtyard almost beneath her window a groom was having problems holding the leading rein of a black, snorting stallion that was dancing on his hind legs.

The first time she had seen him, Francesco had been sitting astride an animal not unlike the one outside. There had been more dust and sweat, but the creature had possessed that same untamed quality…*so had his rider.*

A haziness clouded Erin's cornflower-blue eyes as her thoughts, as though responding to the tug of some invisible magnet, drifted backwards.

She could hear the sound of a horse's hooves clicking on the worn cobbles as it trotted up the steep incline she had had to get off her bike to ascend.

The relief that had rushed through her at the time had been tempered by caution. She was a woman alone. And whose stupid fault was that?

The manager at the hotel had tactfully advised caution when she had explained her intention of hiring a bike to explore the area. When he had realised that none of her three companions was accompanying her he had abandoned tact and expressed his outright disapproval of her plan.

'*Signorina*, it is not a good idea for a woman to travel alone. It is easy to get lost.'

Erin smiled politely, waved her maps at him, and ignored his well-intentioned, and, as it turned out, pretty damned good advice.

She could have explained that she *wanted* to be alone, she absolutely *needed* to be alone; she doubted he would have understood. She didn't really understand herself how women whose company she enjoyed at home could try her patience so totally on holiday. How she had ever imagined they had a lot in common was an even greater mystery!

The fact was if she didn't escape her friends, she might end up telling them what she thought of them, which, although tempting, was out of the question.

They were nice people at home. It was only on holiday they turned into monsters who talked incessantly about their tans and looked at her as though she were insane when she suggested taking a picnic and hiking to the next village.

However, being alone lost its appeal pretty quickly when you found yourself lost with a flat tyre, a burnt nose and aches in muscles you hadn't known you had.

Panic was there just under the surface. A stray thought like, *I'll be a government statistic of tourists who disappeared without trace,* and it would come rushing to the surface.

Well, she wasn't alone anymore.

Erin lifted her hand to shade her eyes from the glare of the strong evening sun. With the sun behind him the figure in the saddle appeared as a dark silhouette outlined by a corona of golden light.

The man saw her and slowed his mount as they approached. The wild-eyed animal, nostrils flared, pawed the ground. Erin, with a mental image of those hooves coming crashing down on her unprotected head, took several hasty steps backwards.

The precaution proved unnecessary as without any apparent effort the rider controlled his animal with nothing more than a soft murmur in fluid Italian and brought it to an abrupt halt.

The horse stood there quivering and the rider sat astride him for what seemed like an age just staring down at Erin until she became frustrated by her inability to see his expression.

Dry-mouthed, she watched warily as he finally kicked his booted feet free of the stirrups and slid off the back of the horse. He patted the creature's quivering flank, sending up a puff of dust, and casually relinquished the reins. The animal pawed the ground restlessly but did not take the opportunity to escape.

Erin, her feet seemingly nailed to the ground and her body reacting at a basic and humiliating level to the undiluted raw sex this stranger exuded from every dusty pore, wondered if the horse, too, was held in thrall as she was.

As he straightened up to his full height it immediately became clear that what she had imagined was an illusion of height created by his vantage point on top of the towering animal was in fact reality!

This man was seriously tall. Tall she could deal with, but the rest was more of a problem! The animal and its master had a lot in common—namely they were both magnificent and indisputably dangerous.

The danger should have repelled her but instead it made her heart beat faster, releasing a flood of adrenaline into her bloodstream. She sucked in a shaky sigh, too awed in that moment to be sensibly wary of this large stranger who exuded a predatory, seductive quality that would normally have had her running for the hills.

She studied him covertly through the screen of her half-lowered lashes. Tall and lean with broad shoulders and narrow hips, he carried himself with the natural grace of an athlete and the casual arrogance of someone who knew that he was one of the beautiful people whose presence alone stopped conversations.

This was the sort of man that she was on principle unimpressed by.

Too good-looking, too sure of himself, he would have been treated from the moment of his birth as if the universe revolved around him.

Strangely as she watched the beautiful stranger peel the leather gloves off his hands she could summon none of the amused contempt she could normally tap into on these occasions.

Maybe it was the leather boots that ended midcalf that were distracting her.

For some reason Erin couldn't tear her eyes off the dusty leather. When she did her gaze travelled up bleached, torn denim and long, *long* legs. She watched, conscious of the sound of her own shallow breathing, as he banged the dust off his thighs. Below the rolled-up sleeves of the shirt he wore open the skin of his strong, sinewed forearms was a deep gold meshed by a dusting of fine dark hair.

He stood there, feet slightly apart, and hooked the leather gloves into the waistband of jeans that were fitted enough to reveal the taut musculature of his powerful thighs and give Erin a hot flush. The black T-shirt he wore beneath his unbuttoned shirt was also snug enough to draw attention to his washboard-flat belly.

Her attention was riveted!

Erin knew she was staring but she couldn't stop. She wanted to move, but her body seemed strangely disconnected from her brain. Her limbs seemed not to belong to her, and inside her chest her heart crashed against her ribcage, almost drowning out the sound of his boots on the cobbles as he walked towards her.

CHAPTER TWO

ERIN swallowed, knowing that this was one of those scenes that would be etched into her mind for ever.

He stopped a few feet away from her but close enough for her to see the dust ingrained in the fine lines radiating from his eyes, extraordinary eyes, incredibly dark and fringed with equally dark curling lashes.

His expression was inscrutable though the groove above his aquiline nose deepened as he looked down at her. Erin felt a shudder chase its way down her spine. There was something almost cruel about the curve of his sensually moulded lips.

He fired a question at her in a deep voice that had an almost tactile quality.

Erin swallowed and lifted her shoulders helplessly to indicate she had no idea what he was talking about.

She saw something that could have been irritation flicker in his dark eyes as he dragged a hand through his hair, which was pitch-black and sheared off at collar level. It was river-straight and she imagined that under the dust it was silky.

Erin could feel her fingertips literally tingling, a disturbing sensation, as she imagined touching…smoothing those dusky strands.

Appalled by the direction of her out-of-control imagination, she concluded that she must have been out in the sun too long. She was probably suffering from dehydration, too, having drained her water bottle an hour earlier.

Rubbing a finger across the bridge of her nose, she was relieved to find evidence to back up her theory. Despite the factor thirty she had plastered on earlier, her skin felt tight and tingly.

Well, it stood to reason that it had to be something like that. She was simply not the sort of woman who went around fantasising about running her fingers through strange men's hair.

Sucking in a deep breath, she adopted an expression that suggested—hopefully—that she was totally immune to tall, romantic-looking figures riding black horses.

'Do you speak English?'

He wasn't the sort of man she would have turned to for help, but she was in no position to be picky.

Actually he was the sort of man that any women with half a brain would cross the street to avoid, though they probably wouldn't, she conceded, recognising the weakness of her own sex when it came to men like this one.

'Eng-lish?' she said, enunciating each syllable slowly in the vain hope of seeing some spark of recognition in his spectacular eyes.

There was none; he just stood there looking as though he'd stepped out of a western.

'I'm lost,' she said, stabbing a finger at her chest.

His eyes followed the action.

'Do you...I need to get to...I'm looking for...damn...!' she muttered, dropping down on her knees and removing the stones she had used to pin the map to the cobbles while she studied it. Anchoring a hank of wayward hair off her face with one arm, she stood up wielding the creased map in the other.

'Map...' she said, waving it at him.

When he looked back at her and shrugged all Erin's frustration bubbled to the surface. The stress of the last few hours manifested itself in tears that spilled down her cheeks. With an angry curse of self-disgust she brushed them away with the back of her hand.

She took a deep breath and told herself to calm down; if this man couldn't help her he might be able to direct her to someone who could.

She smiled encouragingly, then tapped a spot she had ringed in red on the map. 'I need…' she began, lifting her voice to a bellow.

Then she saw the total lack of comprehension in his face and sighed. 'I don't know why I'm shouting. You don't have the faintest idea what I'm talking about, do you?'

He looked from her face to the map in her hands and back again, then gave another magnificent shrug.

Erin's own shoulders sagged. 'Why did you have to be beautiful and stupid? I know several women who would give a lot for your eyelashes. I know several who would give even more for you; there's a very high demand for handsome hunks. I prefer the sensitive types myself, but they tend to be gay.'

His expression didn't alter, though his lips did quiver faintly. Erin gave a guilty sigh.

'Sorry, about this, but while I'm talking I can't panic and if I stop you might go away and I'll be alone again. And the not speaking English, I wasn't serious, it doesn't make you stupid. It would just have been a lot more convenient.

'This is all my fault anyway. I don't know *why* I thought I liked cycling.' She cast a look of loathing in the direction of the discarded bike. 'I wouldn't be surprised if I was saddle sore for a month,' she observed, rubbing a hand over her behind and wincing. 'But the thing is I had to get away from the people I'm on holiday with. I've saved all year for this holiday, but they count carb units at meal times and think local colour is spending the night in a smoke-filled nightclub.' She gave a laugh.

'When you say it like that it doesn't sound so awful, does it? You know, I think the problem is that I'm not very tolerant.' She laughed again and began to fold the map into a more manageable size. 'I know you couldn't care less even if you could understand a word I was saying, but thank you for listening.'

'Any time.'

Her gaze flew upwards and the map fell from her lax grasp. Like the natural fault in a smooth raw silk his deep, cultured voice held an intriguing husk and only the lightest trace of an accent.

'You speak English!' Her initial relief almost immediately morphed into anger. It washed over her in waves as she glared at the impossibly handsome stranger. Her cheeks flamed in mortified horror as she recalled what she had said to him.

He tilted his dark head in acknowledgement and she paled.

God, I called him beautiful!

'Why didn't you say so in the first place instead of letting me babble on?' *And make a total and absolute idiot of myself.*

'I didn't think it was polite to interrupt and once you were in full flow it would have been difficult.'

Erin chose to rise above the provocation, she fixed him with a glare that would have made lesser men wilt and said icily. 'I won't keep you.'

He grinned, displaying a set of even white teeth, and Erin decided the cowboy analogy had been wrong—he was a pirate.

'Don't you think under the circumstances it might be wiser to just suck it in?'

'Suck it in?' she echoed, looking at him in astonishment.

'I'm sure you're entirely self-sufficient in your own neck

of the woods…' He looked at her eyes narrowed, and speculated. 'London?'

'No.'

'Well, wherever it is. This isn't it, *cara*,' he drawled.

The casual endearment caused a spark of anger to flare in her eyes but, more worryingly and fortunately less visible, a quivering liquid heat to unfurl low in her abdomen.

'This is my home territory. You need help and I,' he revealed with an eloquent shrug, 'am it, if you are prepared to put up with my lack of sensitivity.'

'I'm used to insensitive men,' she promised. 'Though none who are quite as sneaky and low as you. And I don't need the cavalry.' She angled a glance towards the horse who stood waiting for his master. 'But if you wouldn't mind telling me exactly where I am I'd be grateful,' she conceded.

One darkly delineated brow lifted to a satirical angle, mockery shone in his expressive eyes.

'If I did would you be any the wiser?'

'Spare me the display of male superiority,' she begged, rolling her eyes. 'In my experience men who go down the "poor little woman couldn't find her way out of a paper bag" route have issues with self-esteem. I am *not* a female stereotype.'

He lifted a hand to shade his eyes as he looked at her. 'Oh, no, you're not that,' he agreed cryptically.

Erin supposed this was her cue to ask exactly what he thought she was, but she had no intention of playing his game. Besides, she wasn't sure that she would like the answer.

She watched as he bent forward to pick up the map. He then smoothed it between his long brown fingers.

His hands, elegant and capable with long, tapering fingers, held a strange fascination for her, and the recognition disturbed her.

He disturbed her.

'That is where you are meant to be?' he said, stabbing the red circle with his finger and slinging her an amused look that oozed the sort of male superiority that made Erin's hackles rise once more.

'I don't suppose you've ever taken a wrong turn,' she snarled sarcastically.

His eyes lifted from the map. 'We're not talking one wrong turn here.' His dry comment confirmed her worst suspicions. 'You're meant to be *here*,' he said, tapping his finger against the spot ringed red.

'I know where I'm *meant* to be—it's where I *am* I want to know,' she retorted waspishly.

'Where you are is not on this map.'

'You mean it's too small?' She had considered the map quite detailed, as far as she could tell marking every tuft of grass.

'I *mean* you're ten miles outside the area it covers, and that is a conservative estimate.'

Her face fell in dismay. 'You're joking,' she said, not actually believing it. This man wouldn't know a joke if he fell over it. 'I—'

'Will you just shut up for a sec and let me think?'

From his expression she suspected that he didn't get told to shut up too often—if ever. Still, she had more important things to worry about than his wounded male Latin pride.

Eyes half closed, her face scrunched in concentration as she considered her options. It didn't take long because she didn't see that she had many. Less if you omitted walking.

'I don't suppose there is such a thing as a taxi around here?'

He looked amused and dug his hand into his pockets, causing the worn fabric to pull taut against his thighs. 'You suppose right.'

She heaved a sigh and tried not to stare too obviously at the muscular thighs. 'Then could you direct me to the nearest phone? I'm sure the hotel will send someone to pick me up.' It would make serious inroads into the money she had set aside for her stay, but what option did she have?

'Where are you staying?'

She mentioned the name of the hotel and his brows rose. 'They pride themselves on being exclusive…'

'And I'm not—?' She could not honestly blame him for coming to this conclusion. By no stretch of the imagination did she look like most people's idea of a well-heeled tourist. 'Actually, you're right. The hotel we were meant to stay in closed because of an outbreak of food poisoning—the tour company upgraded us for free.'

'I'll take you back.'

The abrupt offer made her stare. *'You?'* she said, struggling with an intrusive mental image of herself slung over his saddle riding into the lobby of the exclusive and rather stuffy hotel.

'Do you have a problem with that?'

She had several. 'I really don't think your horse would like it.'

'You're not wrong,' he said, bunching the reins in one hand and patting the animal's flank with the other. 'Actually I know someone who has transport. He only lives a mile or so up the road.'

'That's very kind of you, but—'

'I don't do kind, *cara*.' He smiled and her stomach took an unscheduled dive.

'Are you coming?' He paused, clearly expecting her to fall in step with him.

'I really don't…that is…how?'

He interrupted her with a bored-sounding, 'Is that a yes or a no?'

'No…yes…'

'Are you always this indecisive?'

'I'm sure someone will come if I wait.' Her doubtful tone invited him to disagree.

But he didn't.

Erin watched with mingled astonishment and indignation as he slid a booted foot into a stirrup, and spoke a couple of soothing words to his horse before vaulting with lithe grace into the saddle.

'Well, this is goodbye, then.'

It was only stubborn pride that stopped her begging him not to go. Stubborn pride she had plenty of time to regret during the next twenty minutes.

It took her that long to wheel her bicycle a quarter of a mile up the road where a big rusty truck drew up in a flurry of dust.

CHAPTER THREE

'YOU!' Erin ejaculated in a voice of loathing as the driver got out.

She would have walked back barefoot before admitting even to herself that she was relieved to see him. She supposed her relief stemmed from the fact it really was better the devil you knew even vaguely than any old devil who happened along in a rusty truck.

'So no one came along, then?'

She lifted her chin in response to the mockery in his voice. 'If you traded your horse for that,' she said, nodding with disdain towards the truck, 'you were robbed. The only thing stopping that thing falling apart is rust and dirt.'

There was an amused glint in his dark eyes as they swept the length of her dishevelled figure. 'You're no oil painting yourself, *cara*.'

Erin's lips tightened as the dull colour ran up under her fair skin. It was always ego-enhancing to have an incredible-looking man tell you that you looked a wreck.

His narrowed gaze lingered on her flushed face. 'And that,' he said, casually flicking her nose with his forefinger, 'is going to peel.'

Erin started and pressed her hand to her face. Even if his olive-toned skin had been exposed to the sun it wasn't going to burn, just acquire a deeper glow.

'I hadn't planned on getting lost.' The antagonism died from her flushed face as her dreamily speculative glance drifted to the vee of exposed flesh at the base of his throat.

Was the skin on the rest of his body a similar warm shade? Erin blinked and released a horrified gasp as she realised she had been mentally undressing the man!

Not even sunstroke could excuse that!

'And I hadn't planned on running into you, but life,' he reflected with a sardonic inflection in his deep voice, 'is full of surprises. Some more pleasing than others.'

He didn't specify which category she came into, but Erin could only assume that he had other things he'd prefer to be doing rather than offering assistance to an ungrateful tourist with a red nose.

He walked across to the truck and opened the passenger door. 'Are you getting in?'

Erin's glance slid from the door to his face. She released a sigh and nodded her head. 'I suppose I don't have much choice.'

'There's always a choice.'

Which was exactly what the rational voice in her head, which she had been studiously ignoring, had been telling her. It had also told her that relying on instinct when it came to assessing a man's character was not exactly scientific.

But short of demanding a character reference gut instinct was all she had to go on and she needed to get back to her hotel somehow.

Approaching the truck, she frowned. The cab seemed to be feet off the ground and there were no steps. 'How am I meant to get up there?'

'Like this,' he said, placing both hands around her waist and swinging her off the ground.

Erin let out a startled squeal as she found herself unceremoniously dumped in the passenger seat. She sat there trying to recover her badly dented composure while he picked up her bike and slung it in the open rear of the truck before walking around to the driver's side and climbing in beside her.

'You could have been more careful. The people I hired the bike from are going to charge me if—' She stopped gave a horrified wail and yelled, 'Wait! My camera!'

It was only his restraining hand on her shoulder that stopped her leaping out again.

'Be still.'

Despite her distress at the thought of the camera she could not easily afford to replace being ruined, Erin responded to the calm air of command in his voice and leaned back in her seat.

'Now tell me what is wrong.'

'My camera is in the pannier on the bike.'

'Camera?'

She could tell from his expression that he thought she was making a lot of fuss over a few holiday snaps.

'I'm a photographer and I—'

'Stay there,' he said, opening the door.

Erin stuck her head out of the open window and craned her neck while he climbed into the rear of the truck. A few moments later he returned with her precious camera in his hand. 'Here,' he said, passing it in to her through the open window before going around to the driver's side.

Erin turned her head as he climbed in.

'So you are a photographer?' He didn't sound impressed.

She nodded. 'Nothing grand,' she said, in case he got the

wrong idea. 'I do weddings, christenings, family portraits, that sort of thing…bread-and-butter stuff.'

'So you are not one of that breed who chase celebrities?'

'God, no, nothing like that. I did think once I might like to do more…' She heard the wistful enthusiasm in her voice and stopped. 'Family circumstances keep me close to home.'

'You have a dependent family?'

'Not the way you mean,' she said, thinking that, even had she wanted to, it would have been hard to explain the set-up at home.

Erin had been in her teens before she had realised that other people's fathers did not regularly leave home. She believed the generic term for men like her father was serial adulterer. Jack Foyle always came back suitably contrite, and was always forgiven. But during his absences her mother would go to pieces and become totally unable to cope.

If she hadn't always been there to coax her out of the darkened room and her talk of being unable to go on Erin dreaded to think what would have happened.

She was conscious of his dark eyes on her face as she pretended to examine her camera, but he did not press the point. But then, she reflected, why should he? The domestic circumstances of some accident-prone tourist could hardly interest him.

She flickered a sideways glance in his direction as he turned the ignition. His stern profile was quite stunningly perfect. Ironically he had a face that screamed out to be photographed, though whether any film could capture the raw masculinity he exuded was doubtful.

All the same she would have liked to try.

He turned his head and caught her staring and Erin lowered her gaze.

'There's water somewhere.' He banged a lever with his fist and a door dropped down revealing a bottle of water.

Erin's throat was so dry it hurt and she nodded her thanks. The bottle was ice-cold in her fingers as she lifted it to her mouth and took a long swallow, then with a sigh she rested the cool plastic against her throat.

'Better?'

She turned her head and nodded, then frowned suspiciously as she realised what he was doing. 'Why are you turning around?'

'Because you were going in the wrong direction. Did you really plan to walk all the way back?'

Erin, unwilling to reveal she hadn't actually had a plan, shrugged. 'My friends would have come looking for me eventually.'

'The same friends you had to escape from?'

The reminder that she had used him as a sounding-board to offload all the frustrations made her squirm in her seat and avoid his eyes. 'When I said that I didn't think you could understand me.'

'No, you thought I was beautiful and stupid, but I was forgetting you prefer the *sensitive* types. Do you have one on the scene at the moment?'

Erin, her cheeks burning with embarrassment, glared at him with loathing. 'I'd tell you what I really think of you, but I'm too polite,' she choked. 'Not that you'd know what good manners were if they bit you.'

'You know,' he mused, slowing as they approached a hairpin bend in the road, 'I think you actually like me...' His dark gaze brushed her face. 'You're just in denial.'

Her scornful laugh locked in her throat; his comment was too close to the truth to joke about. 'I'll be in a ditch if you don't keep your eyes on the road.'

'You want to drive?'

Erin shook her head; actually she wanted to sleep. Her muscles, some she hadn't known she possessed, ached from the unaccustomed strenuous physical activity. She slapped her cheeks lightly, fighting to shake the creeping exhaustion that weighed her eyelids.

'If you're tired take a nap.'

Stifling another yawn, Erin turned her head quickly and found he was studying the road ahead. He really was quite spookily perceptive.

'I'm not tired,' she denied brightly.

'Afraid I'll take advantage?'

Under the sweep of her lashes her glance lingered on his upper arms where the fabric of his shirt was stretched taut by the strongly defined muscles. She wrapped her arms around herself as a shivery sensation passed through her body. The fact was, if he decided to take advantage there wasn't a lot she could do about it asleep or awake!

There were some advantages, she reflected, to looking like a survivor in a disaster movie. 'If you're trying to make me feel nervous don't bother…I can take care of myself.'

'Yes, I can see that. I have been staggered by your resourcefulness.' His brows lifted. 'No smart comeback? You must be tired.'

'I'm fine.'

Despite the claim she lost the battle to stay awake a few minutes later.

A hand on her shoulder woke her. Disorientated, she fought her way back to wakefulness, blinking as the dark features of her rescuer swam into focus.

She shot upright in her seat. 'I fell asleep…where?'

Erin opened her gritty eyes fully and saw they were driving through the hotel gates. She stifled a yawn and turned to look at her rescuer; the breath snagged in her throat as his incredible good looks hit her afresh.

She wondered who woke up and saw that face each morning. She knew there had to be someone—this was not a man who slept alone!

Her eyes slid to his left hand.

'No, I'm not married,' he said without looking at her.

Maybe not, but he was spookily perceptive.

'Which makes it all right for you to be interested, *cara*.'

The guilty colour flew to her cheeks. 'I'm not interested!'

His smile was insolent and so confident that she could have screamed. 'Of course you're not,' he drawled.

'My God, you really do think you're God's gift!' she choked in disgust, while privately conceding that he had more justification for thinking it than most men. 'I'm not looking for a holiday romance.'

'I'm not offering you one.'

He drew up beside a Mercedes and, switching off the engine, ignored the red-faced doorman who was waving his arms energetically.

'I think he's afraid you'll lower the tone.'

The possibility appeared not to bother her chauffeur. His long, curling lashes brushed the angle of his cheeks as his gaze slid speculatively over her slim figure. 'I scrub up pretty well,' he revealed modestly. 'Maybe I'll show you some time.'

Erin, conscious of her heart thudding hard behind her breastbone, tried to appear amused by the comment. It wasn't easy when in her head she was seeing him standing naked under the jets of a shower.

Outside on the forecourt a second uniformed figure had joined the near apoplectic footman. Each appeared to be urging the other to approach the truck, but neither seemed too eager to do so. Erin welcomed the diversion.

'I think they,' she said nodding out the window, 'are trying to get your attention.'

His dark eyes remained on her face. 'You have my attention.'

And I so wish I didn't!

Erin swallowed. A wave of heat enveloped her as their gazes meshed. 'Lucky me.'

'As it happens it was lucky for you that I happened by today.'

'Oh, gosh, yes!' She felt stupid for realising that, far from flirting with her, he wanted compensating for his time. A mortified flush spread over her skin. 'Of course I'll pay you for your time and the petrol. My wallet is in my room—if you'll just wait I'll—'

He caught her arm. 'I'm not sure you could afford me…but, no matter, you can have this one on the house.'

She shook her head, very conscious of his cool fingers on her overheated skin… Her skin wasn't the only thing over-heated; her imagination was working overtime. Was the sexual tension she was feeling real or a figment of that imagination?

'Look, I've taken a big chunk out of your day. I'm sure there were other things that you needed to do and—'

'You think I need the money.' The realisation seemed for some reason to amuse him.

Her eyes slid from his.

'Don't worry, I'm a modern man, my male pride can take your pity. Tell you what—how about a compromise?'

'What sort of compromise?' she asked suspiciously.

'You buy me dinner.'

'Dinner!' Her startled eyes flew to his.

He nodded. 'Yes, dinner, at a place of my choice. That's settled, then.'

'*Settled*? I didn't say yes.'

'And you didn't say no. I'll be in touch about our date.'

'It's not a date,' she protested weakly.

'Look, I don't mean to hurry you, but I think I'm about to be thrown out.' He leaned past her and opened the door. He was so close that she could smell the shampoo he used. She closed her eyes as a rush of hormones made her head spin.

When she opened them his face was still close. Their eyes locked and Erin felt things that were way too complicated to be explained by hormones alone.

'Yes,' she whispered in a voice that seemed to be coming from a long way off. 'Yes, I will buy you dinner.'

Taking her chin in his hand, he brushed his lips against hers. The contact was so soft that she barely felt it, but she melted inside.

'My name, *cara*, is Francesco, and I'll be in touch very soon.' He nudged the door so that it swung open and leaned back in his seat.

Conscious of his eyes, Erin fumbled with her belt and jumped out, her knees trembling as she walked towards the building.

He's going to forget you exist the moment he drives away, said the voice in her head.

In retrospect it would have been better that he had.

CHAPTER FOUR

THE minor road Francesco now found himself on was narrow and congested. It was fifteen minutes and several miles later before he found a convenient spot to pull over, a bus stop just on the edge of a village.

There was no breeze and without the air-conditioning running the heat inside the car began to build. Ironically it had been hotter in London when he'd landed than it had been in Rome when he had left. He shrugged off his jacket and wound down the window of the car. It was the first spot of fresh air he'd got since disembarking from his private jet.

Flexing his broad shoulders to relieve the tension that had crept into the muscles, he ran a hand down the curve of his angular jaw, frowning as he felt the dark growth that already cast a visible dusky shadow over his lower face.

As his long brown fingers tugged at the knot of his silk tie he withdrew the phone from his pocket, but before he had flicked it open his attention was captured by raucous cries outside.

He turned his head automatically in the direction of the noise; his dark, curling lashes brushed against perfectly sculpted cheekbones against which his olive-toned skin pulled taut.

His dark glance was disinterested as he looked across to the bus shelter, where a trio of youths were gathered around a girl.

From where he sat Francesco could not see her face, but he could see that she had red hair, the fiery copper-type red that looked like burnished gold in sunlight.

He inhaled sharply, his nostrils flaring in self-derision as he recognised his total inability to control the flood of images that invaded his head. Vivid images that drew his thoughts inexorably backwards until the world around him became less real than that searing kiss. His breath deepened and slowed as the memories took hold.

Erin's soft body was in his arms again, warm, pliant and supple. It was so real he could smell her hair and feel the thud of her heart through the hand he cupped over one small but perfect breast.

Her half-closed passion-glazed eyes, drowning blue and filled with total surrender as she looked up at him, her parted lips a seductive invitation as, warm and sweet-smelling, her breath fluttered against his mouth...

Their date was not going well. During the preceding hours he had thought about kissing her, but not like this! This unpremeditated kiss had been generated partly from sheer frustration. His plan, if such a crazy idea could be couched in those terms, was unravelling before him and, instead of reacting like nine out of ten women, Erin had laughed and acted as though the whole situation were some kind of joke.

Hysteria he could have risen above, but not the infectious giggles that had emerged from her lovely lips as she'd watched him resort to kicking the tyres of the truck.

He had wrenched open the door, furious beyond reason. 'You're a jinx!' he accused, thinking longingly of the Mercedes he had driven out of the city only the previous week.

Francesco was seriously beginning to regret suggesting

the temporary exchange with Ramon, who would be enjoying the benefits of the air-conditioned luxury of that top-of-the-range model.

Considering the situation he now found himself in, Francesco was forced to ask himself if the man who cared for his string of thoroughbred Arabian horses had not had a point when he had questioned his employer's sanity… He could think of several people in the financial circles he moved in who, if they'd been able to see him now, would have had no doubts about it.

Francesco Romanelli, they would have declared, has finally lost it! The only person he could imagine applauding his crazy actions was Rafe, his twin, who, had he still been alive, would have said—*About time!* Though even he might have raised an eyebrow at the extent to which his twin had embraced his new image.

His harsh accusation made Erin stop laughing. 'And you're about as much fun as earache,' she told him frankly.

It took a few moments before he recovered from the shock of being spoken to this way, with none of the respect he automatically took as his due, before he responded.

And that was when he kissed her.

He slid into the driver's seat, leaned across and took her face between his hands. 'You want fun? Fine!' And he lowered his mouth to hers.

The moment their lips touched he lost all control. Nothing that had gone before had prepared him for the searing heat that exploded inside him like a fireball, spreading and consuming him, wiping away every vestige of rational thought and leaving only primal need and hunger.

Nothing that had gone before had prepared him for Erin Foyle!

He could hear her voice in his head, huskily erotic. She said his name as it was wrenched from deep in the heart of her…repeating it over and over, making the syllables sound like a throaty plea as she wound her fingers into his hair, her head thrown back as he kissed the curve of her pale throat.

When they broke apart, both breathing hard, she looked like someone in a trance, her incredible blue eyes glazed and dilated as she looked up at him.

Experiencing a wave of overwhelming tenderness, he cupped her chin, drawing her face up to his, stroking the curve of her soft cheek with his forefinger. The hunger was still there like a prickle under his skin but at least he had it in check.

'I didn't mean to scare you, *cara mia*.' He had done a pretty good job of scaring himself.

She smiled and expelled a shivery little sigh. 'I'm not scared. I'm…' Her voice faltered as she gave a shaky laugh and pressed her hand to the one he held against her face.

He looked at her fingers, small and very pale against his darker skin.

'What are you?'

'All right, I am a little afraid, but not of you,' she added quickly. 'I'm scared of the way you make me feel.' Her eyes fell from his and she looked embarrassed. 'God, that is such an over-the-top thing to say to a total stranger.'

'We're not total strangers.'

Her feathery brows lifted. 'I don't even know your surname.'

'It is Romanelli.' He paused, but there was no flicker of recognition on her face. 'Francesco Luis Romanelli.'

'Well, Francesco Luis Romanelli, I'm Erin, Erin Foyle. I've not the faintest idea what I'm doing here. Why I'm talking to you this way… Why I'm *not* having hysterics because you've just told me we've run out of petrol.' She studied his face as though she expected to find the reason for her aberrant behaviour written there.

After a moment the furrow in her smooth brow relaxed as an impish smile that deepened the dimple in her left cheek spread across her face.

Francesco's hand fell away as she leaned back in the worn leather seat chuckling softly as she drew her knees up to her chin.

'What's so funny?'

'I was thinking about when you walked into the hotel tonight looking like… I thought that waiter, horrid, stuck-up man, was going to have an apoplexy. "We have a strict dress code, sir."' She shook her head. 'Silly man!'

'Looking like what?' he probed, totally hooked by the smile that tugged at the corners of her wide, sweet lips. He hungrily examined the soft contours of her expressive face, finding it hard to believe that twenty-four hours earlier he had never set eyes on her.

'So modest,' she mocked.

'What do you mean?'

'Are you fishing for compliments?'

He shook his head, only half concentrating on her words as he looked at her mouth.

'You strode in there looking like a dark, enigmatic anti-hero, who hides his sensitivity under the surly, brooding exterior.' She laughed at his expression. 'Of course, I know you don't have an ounce of sensitivity because you were quite awful to me yesterday.'

'Yet you are here?'

'Well, you did rescue me.'

'From the results of your own stupidity.'

'Yes, you did touch on the subject of my stupidity yesterday and I agree, in retrospect, that exploring alone that far off the beaten track might not have been the best idea I ever had. But I'm glad I did.'

'You are?' He was amused by her defiance.

She nodded. 'If I hadn't I wouldn't have met you.'

'Perhaps we were fated to meet?' He half expected her to laugh at the suggestion, but she didn't.

'Perhaps…'

'So you came with me tonight out of gratitude?'

'No, not gratitude,' she denied huskily. 'I did promise you a dinner, though I never actually thought I'd see you again.'

'But you wanted to?'

Her eyes slid from his. 'I'm here, aren't I? Are those *exactly* the same clothes you were wearing yesterday?'

'This shirt is clean.' Francesco closed his fingers over her hand and brought it up to his lips. 'And I've showered.'

'But you smelt quite incredibly good yesterday, too.'

'Do you always say exactly what you are thinking?'

She looked startled by the question. After a thoughtful pause she shook her head. 'No, it's just with you. That's really strange, don't you think?'

Not nearly so strange, Francesco thought, as a man who could command a private jet simply by picking up a phone pretending to be the owner of a truck that most people would have been embarrassed to be seen in.

'This is probably the most irresponsible thing I've done in my life,' she admitted. 'I suppose you've done a lot of irresponsible things?'

'You sound envious.'

'A little.'

'Your friends didn't look happy when you came with me.'

'They weren't; they think I have lost my mind,' she admitted frankly. 'They suspect you prey on silly, impressionable female tourists like me. They think your intentions are dishonourable.'

'Your friends are right—my intentions are entirely dishonourable.'

She blushed a little, but did not drop her gaze from his. 'I'm relieved to hear it. They were actually green with jealousy.'

'Perhaps,' he suggested, playing devil's advocate, 'they had your best interests at heart. You know, I didn't intend it to be like this.' His frustrated scowl encompassed the borrowed beat-up truck.

'I feel quite insulted. I thought running out of petrol was some elaborate plan to seduce me,' she pouted. Behind the teasing words and smile her eyes still held that dazed, bruised quality.

'I did have a plan to seduce you, but it wasn't this.'

'Was your plan nice?'

'It depends how you feel about candlelight and silk sheets.' And a meal served by an internationally renowned chef who had been flown in from Paris for the occasion on his private jet.

'Oh, that was very sweet. Why are you laughing?'

'I've never been called sweet before,' he admitted.

'Well, you are *very*, in a wolfish sort of way. You know, there is an upside to this situation.'

'There is?'

'I've never made love in a car. Actually, I've never…' She stopped and spoiled the bold invitation by giggling nervously as if surprised by her own audacity.

He caught hold of the small hand and pressed her palm to his lips. The shudder that rippled through her body was visible. He imagined how she would respond to a more intimate touch and realised that he was shaking with anticipation as much as she was.

'This is not a car,' he said, thinking about how she would taste when he ran his tongue down the valley between her breasts.

'No, there's much more room. And you shouldn't be embarrassed,' she added, her expression growing earnest. 'I'm not the sort of girl who's impressed by flashy cars, Francesco, and what would you need with a flashy car? You work with horses and you couldn't fit a bale of hay or something in the back of a Porsche.'

'How do you know I work with horses?'

'You mean you don't?'

It was at that point that Francesco chose to lie, telling himself she'd laugh when he revealed the real truth. And it wasn't as if it were an outright lie—as often as his hectic schedule would allow he tried to spend time training the horses on his estate, which had been in his family since the thirteenth century. He had come there more frequently of late, feeling the need to escape from conversations that stopped abruptly when he walked into a room.

'Anyway, it's a well-known fact men who drive those sort of cars have something to compensate for.'

'Is that so?' he said, thinking of the several gleaming models, including a Porsche, sitting idly in his own garage.

'You don't think I have anything to compensate for? You wouldn't prefer me if I had money and could afford to take you to a smart hotel?'

There was a long silence while she just gazed up at him. 'I like you just the way you are.'

Unable to resist any longer, he bent forward, framed her face between his hands and kissed her with the same combustible results!

'*Dio mio!*' he groaned, dragging his head away. 'We're here for the world to see!'

Undeterred by the lack of privacy, she continued to press hot, hungry kisses to the damp skin of his throat while her trembling fingers fumbled with the buttons of his shirt.

'We should wait.'

'Just thinking about you makes me ache deep inside,' she confided huskily.

Francesco groaned. 'Do you have any idea what you're doing to me?'

Her breasts strained against the silk of her blouse as she gave a shuddering sigh in response to his throaty confession. 'Do you know how totally beautiful you are, Francesco?' She traced a line down his sweat-dampened skin from his throat all the way to the waistband of his trousers. 'Of course you do, but I'm trying not to think about all the—'

'We are neither of us thinking.' The effort of will required to remove the small hand that was tugging at the buckle of his belt made him physically shake like someone in the grip of a fever.

Her searing blue passion-glazed eyes lifted to his face. 'Did I get it wrong? I thought you said you intended to seduce me.'

'*Dio mio*…I did…I do…but not here. I wanted it to be special the first time.'

'"The first time…"' she echoed, laughing.

Later the laughter had made sense.

'There was a farm a mile or so back. I will walk back and get petrol.'

'Is there anything I can do to make you change your mind?' she asked, shooting him a provocative look from beneath the sweep of her lashes as she began to unfasten the buttons of her blouse.

As the heaving upper slopes of her creamy breasts were exposed his control snapped and he pulled her roughly into his arms.

'Thank God!' she breathed into his mouth as they slid down in the seat.

She had been so totally uninhibited about expressing her pleasure at his touch that Francesco had not suspected until the actual moment he slid into her body and heard her tiny cry of shock that she had still been a virgin.

He was both appalled and aroused by the knowledge that he was her first lover.

'Relax, let me make this good for you,' he begged huskily as she arched beneath him and slid her hands across his bare shoulders, clinging on as though she feared she would fall.

'Oh, my God, you're just incredible, Francesco!'

The hoarse cries of astonished pleasure he was hearing in his head mingled with the more high-pitched sounds of laughter that drifted in through the window. Sucking in a deep breath through flared nostrils, Francesco dragged his thoughts kicking and screaming back to the present.

It took several moments for him to get the hunger that still roared like a furnace in his veins under control.

He sighed and dragged a hand through his hair. Reaching inside the glove compartment, he pulled out Erin's letter. He slowly tore it in half, then in half again before throwing it out the open window. The gesture was purely symbolic, but it made him feel better to watch the pieces scatter as a gust of wind caught them.

CHAPTER FIVE

FORGETTING about the phone call he had intended to answer, Francesco was about to turn the ignition when there was more laughter outside. And mingled with this laughter was a tearful cry that held an unmistakable note of fear.

Frowning, he turned his head at the same moment one of the youths moved and he saw the girl's face; underneath the overdone make-up that caked her face she was very young. The terror he saw written clearly in the childish features radically changed the situation. This was not simply high spirits.

With a sigh he opened the door. The fact was he didn't need any of this, but Francesco had not been brought up to turn a blind eye and ignore his duty and social responsibility.

The youths were too busy, and, if the beer cans discarded on the floor were any indicator, too drunk to register his presence until he was right upon them.

'I think the lady would like to leave.'

As one they swung around to face him, their expressions uniformly smug and belligerent. The one who was obviously the self-appointed leader dug his thumbs into his belt and took a swaggering step towards Francesco who, rather than recoiling in horror as he was meant to, simply looked bored.

This reaction visibly troubled the glassy-eyed gang leader.

'Who asked you?'

Francesco smiled. It was a smile that sent a cold shudder down the young boy's spine.

'Why don't you boys just run along home, no harm done?' Francesco suggested pleasantly.

The youth nearest raised a can to his mouth and drained it before mangling the tin in his hand and flinging it over his shoulder. '*We're* not running no place, mate!' he announced loudly. 'So why don't you mind your own business?'

The pathetic bravado was wasted on Francesco, who was fast losing his patience. He lifted one hand, flicked the cuff of his jacket and glanced at the metal-banded watch that glittered against his olive-toned skin. He had places to be and his plan to reach there before lunch was beginning to seem optimistic.

'That is, of course, your choice, but the young lady—' he nodded towards the scared-looking teenager '—would like to go home. Is that not so?'

The young girl nodded and eagerly ran into the shelter offered by his outstretched arm. 'You are all right?' Francesco asked softly.

The girl who looked up at him as though he was her saviour nodded and wiped the tears from her cheeks, smearing mascara over her face in the process. Looking at her more closely, Francesco realised that beyond the vibrant hair she bore no resemblance whatsoever to his wife.

For a start the woman he had married would not have cringed in a corner while brainless thugs intimidated her. One corner of his mouth lifted into a wry half-smile as he contemplated her probable actions if she found herself in a similar situation.

His redhead would have stuck out her chin and ripped her attackers apart with her rapier-sharp tongue. And if that hadn't been sufficient she would have aimed some kicks at their most vulnerable areas, and most likely landed a few.

Neither would she have welcomed his well-meant intervention. No, she would have told him in no uncertain terms that she was more than capable of taking care of herself.

'I think it's time you went home,' he suggested gently to the girl, who did not resent his interference.

She did not require a second bidding. Casting him one last look of supreme gratitude, she fled.

'I don't think so,' Francesco said, turning his body to block the youth who had moved to pursue her.

'But she liked me…'

Francesco smiled. 'Did you not know? It is a lady's privilege to change her mind, and a gentleman always remembers that.'

Folding his long, lean length into the driver's seat, Francesco dismissed the incident from his mind almost immediately, or most of it anyway. But the hair kept triggering memories he fought to keep in check for the rest of the journey.

Valentina tracked her guest down to the small sitting room. The south-facing room was her own favourite in the big rambling house that had become her home when she had left her native Tuscany to marry her English husband five years earlier.

She glanced at her watch before hitching her infant son a little more securely onto her hip. Her expression was reluctant as she reached for the door handle.

Half an hour earlier her husband had revealed the details of his master plan. She had seen the flaws immediately.

'What if she doesn't *want* to be in the library at eleven-thirty?' she asked. 'What if Francesco is late? What am I meant to do then?'

'You'll think of something, and if Francesco says he is going to be here at a certain time he will be.'

Valentina could not deny his last point. People who meant *exactly* what they said were rare, but her cousin was one of them.

'You know, Sam, I think you're enjoying this cloak-and-dagger stuff far too much!'

She, on the other hand, was having serious misgivings. When she expressed her doubts about being part of what amounted to a conspiracy, Sam dismissed her concerns.

'Conspiracy? This isn't a *conspiracy*, Val.'

'Well, what would you call it? We invited Erin to a party that doesn't exist, when we're actually going to lock her in a room with her estranged ex!'

'There will be no *locking* involved. I've just made sure that they can have the house to themselves for a few hours.'

'Erin will probably never speak to me again,' Valentina predicted gloomily.

'We're just helping two people get back together,' Sam soothed. 'Look at it this way—does Erin *look* happy?'

'Couldn't he just pick up a telephone like anyone else?'

'Once the lawyers get involved things get complicated.'

'Maybe, but *why* does he want to see her?'

'Well, obviously he wants to try again. He wants reconciliation. What other reason could there be?'

Valentina did not even attempt to explain about the complexities of Latin male, macho pride to her English husband. As much as she loved Francesco, she was not blind to his faults; her cousin was capable of being utterly ruthless.

Of course, it might be as simple as Sam suggested; he might just want to salvage his marriage. The problem was, where Francesco was concerned things were rarely simple!

'Look, I really don't see what the problem is. Francesco has asked for our help. When did he ever do that?'

'Never,' she admitted.

Her charismatic cousin was just about the most self-sufficient individual she had ever encountered. He was the type of person that people instinctively turned to in times of crisis. A cloud passed over her face as her thoughts turned to the tragedy that had recently devastated the Romanelli family.

Rafe, Francesco's twin brother, had taken his own life.

She was ashamed to admit, but she had been so caught up in her own grief that she had spared very little thought to how Francesco, who had remained a tower of strength throughout, must be feeling.

Then on the day of funeral she had walked into a room and found him alone. At the sound of his name Francesco had lifted his head...the bleak despair she had seen in his eyes during that brief unguarded moment would stay with her for ever.

The family had considered it a good thing when he had thrown himself into his work with even more energy than usual, but she hadn't been so sure.

So when after weeks of being pretty elusive Francesco had telephoned out of the blue and announced he was getting married Valentina had been delighted for him.

A secret ceremony in a tiny chapel with only herself and Sam to witness the event had seemed the height of romance until she'd realised the couple had only met five days earlier!

That had really set the alarm bells ringing!

It was hard not to conclude, given the timing, that his totally out-of-character whirlwind marriage had been some sort of backlash to his twin brother's death.

She hadn't really been surprised when the marriage had folded after a month.

'I for one,' Sam added, 'would do a hell of a lot more than tell a few white lies for him. He believed in me when nobody else did, or have you forgotten how much we owe him? We'd have lost this house…the stud, everything!'

'I know…I know…and I'd do anything for him *normally*, but we're *lying* to Erin. How's she going to feel when she realises we've been tricking her?'

In the end they'd come to a compromise: she would not spill the beans to Erin, but if the other girl asked her a direct question she wouldn't lie.

CHAPTER SIX

ERIN, who was curled up on the sofa, put the book she was reading to one side and rose to her feet when Valentina walked in.

'Who were you talking to?' Valentina asked, looking around the empty room.

'The heroine,' Erin explained, indicating the book that lay open. 'She is so *good* it makes me nauseous.'

'Then why are you reading the book?'

'I'm hoping she'll wake up and realise that the hero she's been waiting for doesn't exist.' The problem with heroic-looking men was it was a massive disappointment when you discovered they were just as incapable of knowing the meaning of fidelity as any other man.

'That makes you a terrible cynic.'

'That makes me an optimist,' Erin retorted, running a hand through her hair before tightening the knot in the orange scarf that secured it in a loose ponytail at her nape. The vibrant colour clashed gloriously with the equally vibrant shade of her copper-red curls. 'She might not be as stupid as she seems.'

Her glance drifted to the plump baby gurgling contentedly in his mother's arms. Valentina made motherhood look so easy…just watching her made Erin feel inadequate. Were good mothers born or could you learn? she wondered…

Erin hoped, for the sake of her unborn baby, that the latter was true!

'So, being an optimist, do you think people can change?'

Erin tore her eyes from the golden-skinned baby and caught Valentina watching her with an expression that made her wonder uneasily if she didn't suspect something. It wasn't the first time she had received that impression.

For a moment Erin was tempted to tell her; she ached to have someone to confide in, someone to tell her that the doubts and fears that kept her awake nights were normal.

But then sanity intervened.

Francesco was Valentina's cousin and to ask her to keep the information from him would put her in an awful position. Valentina would no doubt consider that Francesco had a right to know and Erin could not disagree, she knew she had to tell Francesco about the baby.

She had actually been on the point of putting pen to paper to do just that earlier that week, not having mentioned it in her earlier letter, when she had picked up the phone and without warning heard his voice.

But when the moment had presented itself, she hadn't told him; she hadn't said anything.

She hadn't been able to—the protective defences she had struggled to construct had disintegrated and so had she! Her eyes had still been puffy and red the next day from the orgy of weeping just hearing his voice had triggered.

It would be so much simpler if her conscience would allow her to delay telling him until after the divorce. Because once he did know Erin knew that realistically there would be no question of a smooth, uncontested divorce.

It just wasn't going to happen.

Not given Francesco's inflexible and unforgiving attitude when it came to the subject of fathers who tried to evade their responsibilities.

Francesco held the view that absentee fathers came slightly lower on the evolutionary scale than lice! And while he had once expressed some admiration for single mothers who brought up children and juggled careers, he had added the rider that it was inevitable the child would suffer.

The moment he knew about the baby Erin *knew* that he would use all his considerable powers of persuasion to make her give up the idea of a divorce completely.

But even if he had turned up on his knees begging her to come back, a scenario slightly less likely than snow in the desert, Erin would not have considered trying again, especially only for the sake of their unborn child.

It wasn't as if it would work out any better the second time around. Nothing had changed. Essentially they were the same people, the same totally incompatible people. If they got back together she would only end up having to walk away a second time.

And that was something she had to avoid at all costs. Leaving the first time had hurt more than anything in her life and the thought of feeling pain like that again… *Oh, my God, I just can't go through that again!* she thought, gulping as she bent to pick up the stuffed toy Gianni had thrown on the floor.

'No, I don't think people can change,' she said, putting the toy back in the baby's plump hand.

In order to change you had to admit you were in the wrong—something that her estranged husband had refused point-blank to do. As her thoughts lingered on the subject of Francesco her soft features grew bleak.

It wasn't difficult to work out what she had seen in him. He had had more raw sexual magnetism in his little finger than a normal man had in his entire body.

Erin could forgive herself for the physical attraction, but what she couldn't forgive herself for was seeing emotional depth in his brooding silences and strength in his reticence.

It seemed laughably pathetic now, but she had really thought she had found her soul mate, the one man in the world that she was meant to be with. She had seen what she wanted, when in reality there had been nothing to see.

He had been shallow, selfish and cruel.

How had she ever imagined that their marriage could work?

She was confident that walking out and turning her back on him and a lifestyle to which she had been patently unsuited had been the right thing to do. She had no doubts at all…if only she could forget that look of bleak devastation she had seen in his dark eyes…

'But sometimes…' Valentina's voice interrupted her thoughts.

Erin shook her head. 'My mum believed my dad could change for thirty years.'

It was the first reference that Erin had made to her parents' marriage. On the one occasion Valentina had met Erin's mother, she had been far less restrained when it came to disclosing the gory details of her husband's numerous infidelities! Much to her daughter's obvious discomfiture.

'When you were growing up…did you know what was going on?' Valentina asked curiously.

Erin shrugged, her expression tight as she admitted, 'The entire village knew what was going on.'

Valentina gave a grimace of sympathy. She herself had found it difficult to warm to Clare Foyle. She couldn't rid herself of the uncharitable conviction that the older woman rather enjoyed her status as tragic, dumped wife.

What Erin still struggled to understand was that, after all these years and numerous affairs, all her father had to do was look sheepish and contrite and his wife would welcome him with open arms no matter how many times he humiliated her.

Erin knew better than to challenge her father or attempt to make her mother see he would ever change. The only thing her previous interventions had never done was make her mother accuse her of not wanting to see her happy.

She gave a philosophical mental shrug. She had long ago accepted that where her father was concerned her mother could not think rationally.

And who was she to criticize? Hadn't she almost gone down the same road herself?

'They're planning a trip to France to tour the wine-making regions.'

'My cousin married an Australian winemaker…' Valentina stopped and gave a self-conscious grimace. 'But then you'd know that. Sorry, I didn't mean to…'

'No need to be sorry,' Erin said, pretending a pragmatism she was a million miles away from achieving. 'And actually there are entire chunks of Francesco's life which are a total mystery to me.'

'Well, I don't suppose that is so surprising—you actually didn't know one another very long. That isn't a criticism,' she added quickly. 'Sam said he knew he was going to marry me five minutes after we met!'

'But I'm assuming that you waited a little longer than five days before you got married.'

Most sane people did, she reflected, still unable three months after the event to explain the reckless way she had jumped into marriage with a man whom she hardly knew. A man who she had already discovered had lied more than once to her.

But then there had not been a whole lot of sanity involved in her steamy relationship with Francesco Romanelli!

'This entire divorce thing is going to be a total nightmare. I wish we could just do it without involving a lawyer. I really don't care about the money…I just want to put it all behind me, but Mum says…' Erin shrugged and bit her lip. 'She never really took to Francesco,' she admitted.

Valentina suspected that Clare Foyle would never take to any man who took away the daughter she used as an emotional prop, but she maintained a tactful silence.

The baby in her arms began to cry. 'Gianni is a bit cranky today.'

Erin ran a tentative finger down the baby's soft cheek, swallowing past the emotional lump in her throat. 'He's a lovely baby,' she observed huskily. 'You're very lucky.'

Valentina nodded. 'I know,' she admitted. 'So shall we go find Sam? I think he's in the library.'

'Library?'

'Yes, he's dying to take you on a tour of the stud,' she said, taking Erin's arm and steering her towards the door.

'That would be interesting,' Erin admitted, puzzled by her hostess's urgency. 'But I wouldn't want to be an imposition. Couldn't I give you a hand?'

Valentina looked blank. 'A hand?'

'Well, aren't the other guests arriving this morning?'

'Everyone who's coming should be here by eleven-thirty, but everything's under control.'

Her strained smile made Erin suspect that organising the weekend had been more fraught than Valentina had anticipated.

'I'm sure everything will go smoothly,' Erin said soothingly.

For some reason this comment drew a nervous laugh from her increasingly anxious-looking hostess.

Valentina paused, her hand on the door of the library. 'I was wondering…' she began.

'You were wondering what?'

'I was wondering if you're really serious about this divorce thing…I know it's none of my business.'

'I'm deadly serious.'

Valentina sighed. 'Well, I think it's sad. You and Francesco on your wedding day looked so…you looked so *right* together.'

Erin swallowed the lump in her throat. She remembered how it had *felt right* when his mouth had covered her own. How right it had felt when they had lain skin to skin touching…but sometimes, she reflected grimly, instincts were wrong. What felt right was anything but!

'Sometimes things don't work out,' she said lamely; she could hardly bad-mouth Francesco to his cousin.

Actually she hadn't bad-mouthed him to anyone, and bizarrely there had been more than one occasion when she had even found herself defending him in the face of her mother's savage criticism. Well, whatever else he was, Francesco was the father of her unborn child.

'Sam and I had some spectacular rows when we first married,' Valentina revealed candidly. 'Living with someone even when you love them can be difficult in the early days.'

'Look, I appreciate what you're saying,' Erin said. 'But you and Sam…well, it isn't comparing like with like. Did Sam ever pretend to be someone he wasn't? Did you have to learn by accident that the man you were marrying the next day was someone quite different?'

Valentina, looking confused, shook her head. 'You didn't know who Francesco was?'

'Well, I didn't know he was some filthy-rich banker with a family tree that can trace itself back to the year dot, and I'd be grateful if you tell that to anyone who suggests I married him for his money.'

'Nobody thinks that!' Valentina exclaimed, horrified by the suggestion.

'I've no doubt they will,' Erin retorted as her thoughts were dragged inexorably back to the moment when she had accidentally discovered the true identity of her future husband.

She had experienced no flicker of premonition as she had picked up a paper that had wafted onto the floor from the desk piled high with Francesco's files.

The letterhead on the heavy vellum paper had pronounced it came from the Romanelli Bank.

She remembered being struck by the coincidence of Francesco doing business with a bank that had his own name. It had been a sudden concern, not suspicion, that had made her go back and study it. Why did banks write to people?

What if Francesco had financial problems? She had had to remonstrate with him on more than one occasion about his generosity.

Guiltily she had skimmed the typewritten letter. The convoluted wording and technical language it was couched in meant she hadn't understood one word in five, but one thing she had understood was the signature at the bottom of the page.

She would have recognised that distinctive bold flourish anywhere.

What was Francesco's name doing at the bottom of a letter from a bank?

She had suddenly remembered an incident that had not seemed important at the time. It had been the first time he had driven her up to his remote home two days earlier. On the way she had pointed at the name plaque on a large automated gate and laughingly asked if that was where he lived.

'Romanelli is a common name around here.'

Around the next bend she caught a fleeting glimpse of a vast honey-coloured stone building that resembled a fairy-tale castle.

'The people who live there must be very rich,' she commented.

'They own the estate.'

'Is it large?'

'Many thousands of acres.'

Of course, she forgot the rich people in their castle when he brought her to his home. Though only half the conversion was completed, Francesco's home, which he explained he was converting with his own hands, totally enchanted her.

It was a perfect marriage of rustic and contemporary. All the materials, he proudly explained, were locally sourced, many reclaimed from other old buildings which had fallen into disrepair.

Francesco's plans for the place were ambitious.

'When it is finished there will be a glass corridor linking the two wings and that gable end will be glass.'

'It's beautiful, Francesco,' she said, her imagination fired by the picture he drew.

'It is perfectly habitable at the moment. Is it somewhere you could imagine living?'

'I'll never live anywhere half so beautiful.'

'You could.'

'You mean for the rest of my holiday?'

'I mean stay here. Live here with me?'

The request startled her, but she still did not understand the sigificance. 'You mean permanently? But I have a job, a life…I…'

'You misunderstand. I am asking you to marry me.'

Thinking of that castle, she had opened his laptop.

A few moments later the Internet had confirmed her suspicions.

Erin had confronted him immediately.

She had expected him to be defensive and perhaps annoyed that she had gone behind his back, but Francesco had been totally relaxed about the entire thing.

'Quite the little detective,' he murmured indulgently.

'But you said that you work with horses.'

'And so I do. I did not lie to you. I just do other things, too.'

'Like make lots of money.'

'So long as I have enough to support a family I don't see that the state of my bank balance is relevant.'

Not relevant? She stared at him in disbelief. 'But *you own the bank*! Your name is in the first column of the European Rich List. You can trace your family tree back to royalty.'

'Well, you can see why I don't shout it from the rooftops, can't you? You tell people you are a banker and they begin to yawn straight away.'

'This is not a joke, Francesco. Things are going too fast.'

'Then let us be serious for a moment. I do not own a bank— my family, and specifically my father, does. Money is a by-product of what I do, but it is not intrinsically important to me.'

'But it's not just the money. You have a family, Francesco. Do they even know about me?'

'My family will love you, *cara*,' he purred in his sinfully sexy voice.

She felt her anger slip away as he tangled his fingers into

the mesh of her hair, massaging his fingers into her scalp. He tilted her head back and kissed her.

A long, tremulous sigh left her lips when his head lifted.

'My parents are staying with my sister in Australia. I have contacted them and told them about our marriage. They are ringing this evening to speak to you. They can't wait to meet you. They would have flown back but my mother had an accident—nothing serious, but she cannot make the trip.

'They have had some sad times recently. You will bring some joy into their lives. As you have brought joy into mine,' he said, holding her face in his hands and staring down at her with an expression that made her traitorous heart skip a beat.

'But shouldn't we wait until they get back? I don't understand the hurry.'

'I really can't wait that long, *tesoro mio,* to make you my wife. Afterwards,' he promised with a shrug, 'they can arrange anything they wish, but you will be mine.'

Valentina's hand on her arm cut through Erin's brooding recollections.

As she walked through the door Valentina stopped and turned to face Erin. 'Look, Erin, I know what this seems like,' she began urgently.

Erin shook her head in total bewilderment. 'What seems like?'

'I'm really sorry.'

'Sorry about what?'

Valentina shook her head, her gaze trained on a point in the room beyond Erin. Erin automatically turned.

She literally felt the blood drain from her face.

Her body responded to the sight of the tall, supremely elegant figure who stepped forward, impeccable in his light grey suit and open-necked white shirt, exactly the same way it would have to a couple of thousand volts of neat electricity.

For a split second every nerve cell in her body fired off then shut down.

She stared at him, her throat aching with the emotions locked there. An irrational part of her visualised flinging herself into his arms and she really had to fight against her genetic predisposition to do so. It would mean heartbreak all over again.

She would not let history repeat itself. One woman in the family prepared to humiliate herself to keep a man was more than enough.

This can't be happening now. I'm not ready to do this yet.

The same sexual awareness that she had always experienced in his presence hummed in her bloodstream; it made it impossible to think rationally. It always had—that was the problem.

He was standing only a couple of feet away from her at the most. If she had reached out she could have touched him, laid her hand on his chest and felt the warmth of his skin, the thud of his heartbeat.

A strange little laugh emerged from her lips. Losing composure scarily fast, she turned her head. Her gaze met that of Valentina, who grimaced at the silent reproach in her eyes.

The older woman shook her head and mouthed, *I'm sorry*.

'You planned this.' The sense of betrayal Erin felt was intense.

She had been genuinely touched that Francesco's cousin had made an effort to cultivate friendship even after what had happened.

'Francesco just wanted to talk to you and…we meant it for the best.'

Sam, who had come to stand behind his wife, placed a hand on her shoulder. 'Come on, sweetheart. Let's leave them to it.' As he took his infant son from her arms he looked directly at Erin. 'Val didn't want to do this.' He glanced towards Francesco, nodded almost imperceptibly, and guided his wife from the room.

CHAPTER SEVEN

FOR several seconds after the door closed Erin did not move or react. The silence in the room screamed.

The only way she had survived their separation was by recognising that she no longer loved Francesco. That she never actually had. *Real* love, the sort that endured, was slow burning. It had nothing to do with the dark, sizzling heat and mind-numbing lust their marriage had been based on, but was about shared interests and mutual respect.

Mutual respect, she muttered through clenched lips. It was a necessary reminder. It would be perilously easy to allow chemistry to confuse her when every cell in her body was reacting to him standing there.

She could be sexually attracted to him—who wouldn't be? But attraction didn't equate with deeper feelings.

It equated with disaster!

Concentrate, she told herself, *and don't think about his mouth. Concentrate on what a total bastard he is and getting out of this room without making a total fool of yourself...that and breathe.*

Yes, breathing would be useful. She tilted her chin and took a deep, steadying breath, schooling her stiff features into what she hoped was an expression of contempt.

'This is a pretty low trick, Francesco, even by your standards.'

Eyes trained on her face, he gave a very Latin shrug. 'I had no alternative.'

Before she had walked into the room he had been angry. Now she was here and he was still angry, but interwoven with the anger were tenacious threads of tenderness. Hands clenched, he ruthlessly subdued a sudden strong compulsion to cradle her in his arms. Under the hostility she looked so damned fragile!

The groove above his masterful nose etched deep as his eyes continued to rake her face.

Some might have considered the recent changes in her appearance were subtle, but not Francesco, who had every line and curve of her face committed to memory.

The alterations screamed at him. Her face was thinner, emphasising the delicate bone structure and making her eyes appear even bigger, and there was a haunted quality in their bright jewellike depths. Her skin still had that fabulous translucent quality, but there were fine lines of strain around her wide mouth.

Were these visible signs of strain the results of a difficult pregnancy? He had to clamp his teeth over the angry demands for information that hovered on his tongue.

Her lips twisted and Erin shook her head in weary disbelief. There wasn't even a hint of apology in his manner. *And you're surprised?* she taunted herself.

'No alternative but to lie and cheat—now why aren't I surprised?' she drawled.

A flash of anger ignited the gold highlights deep in his dark eyes. 'You would not take my calls, Erin.'

The way he said her name always had caused her stomach muscles to flutter. It still did, though as there was a lot of quivering going on it was hard to separate out the disturbing sensation from all the others.

'You refused my request for a face-to-face meeting.' The steel in his manner was more pronounced as his dark eyes narrowed in recollection.

'Call singular,' Erin countered coldly.

'You can relax, Francesco I don't want your money, if that's what you're worried about.'

Erin permitted herself a bitter smile as she wondered what her mother would say if she had heard this statement.

Far from responding to her scornful rejection of his fortune with any sign of visible relief, Francesco merely dismissed her.

'Money? I have no interest in money. I have not been calling you every day to talk about money.' His hands clenched at his sides as he struggled to contain his sense of outrage.

'*Every day!* Now I know that's not true,' she told him, appalled at this outright and not terribly imaginative lie.

For the first week after she had returned to England she had fully expected him to turn up. She had pretty much lived in dread…well, about half the time had been dread. The shameful fact was the other fifty per cent of the time her feelings had more accurately fallen under the heading of eager, impatient even, sweaty-palmed, heart-thudding anticipation of opening the door and finding him standing there.

But as it turned out there had been no occasion for her to use her specially prepared speech, the one that made allowances for his feelings. It had been humiliating, but in the long run she had told herself a very important lesson.

She had made the mistake of assuming that he wanted their marriage to continue. That he wanted her. And he hadn't even picked up a phone to ask her to come back, to say that he missed her.

The answer was simple, of course, though it had taken her long enough to work it out: he didn't miss her. He had simply written off their marriage, put it down to experience and picked up the threads of his life…carried on being important and dynamic and stopping conversations when he walked into a room.

'When I rang, your mobile was switched off.'

'I lost the old phone, I think. I don't know where it is.' The days immediately following her return to England two months earlier were still something of a blur to her.

Before she could put a name to the flare of emotion that spilled from his dark eyes, Francesco's heavy lids lowered concealing his expression under the thick mesh of his lashes. 'That was careless of you.'

Erin gave a wistful little smile and placed a hand lightly to her belly. 'Even when you're careful, accidents happen.'

'Did you have any accident in particular in mind?'

The edge in his deep accented voice brought her wary glance upwards. 'What do you mean?' she demanded shrilly.

One dark brow lifted to a sardonic angle. 'Defensive, Erin?'

The suggestion brought a guilty flush to her cheeks. 'No…I just meant accidents, accidents in general.' The retort sounded pathetically lame even to her own ears so she was surprised and relieved when Francesco didn't comment on it.

Instead he explained tautly, 'I have been ringing your home number several times a day for the past four days—your mother told me you did not wish to speak to me.'

'My mother!' she echoed, an audible thread of uncertainty entering her voice. 'But she…' She stopped and bit her lip.

It was entirely possible he spoke the truth. Her mother's antagonism for the man her daughter had married had been instant and the feeling had been mutual. The overnight visit they had made to break the news to her parents in person the week after the wedding had been a total disaster.

Her mother had gone to pieces when Erin had gently explained that she would be moving to Italy, and Francesco had not helped matters by not being at all sympathetic to her distress.

When she had taken him to task over his attitude in private he had informed her that her mother would soon find someone else to take her place as an emotional prop.

'She is playing on your guilt, but what do you have to feel guilty about?' he asked her.

'I don't feel guilty,' Erin protested.

'You are not responsible for your parents. It's time you realised that they stay in their marriage, not because they have to, but because it suits them both.'

Recalling the conversation now ignited the resentment Erin had felt at the time.

'Yes, I spoke to your mother. She has explained in some detail how the mention of my name makes you feel sick and the only thing keeping you going is the thought of taking me for all I'm worth.'

'And you believed her!' It made her angry that he could consider her capable of being so mercenary.

'Was she not following your instructions?' He shook his head incredulously and loosed a bitter laugh. 'Believed her? One thing you are *not* guilty of, *cara*, is avarice!' His eyes dropped and it seemed to a horror-struck Erin that he was staring at her still-flat stomach.

My God, he knows about the baby...!

She froze, her eyes wide and shocked, the colour leaking from her face. Common sense reasserted itself about a heartbeat later. A shaky sigh of relief escaped her lips as she recognised her guilt-fuelled imagination was making her read things into his expression and body language that weren't there.

Francesco couldn't possibly know, unless he was a mind-reader. Nobody but her doctor knew and she wasn't showing yet. In fact after the weeks of vile morning sickness she weighed less than she had ever done.

She allowed the hands she had instinctively brought up in a protective gesture to casually fall from her middle. 'I won't ask what I am guilty of.'

'Your mother didn't tell you about the calls?'

Her eyes slid from his. 'I expect Mum was just trying to protect me.'

'From me?' A muscle in his lean check clenched.

Erin's head lifted. 'It's what mothers do.'

'Not yours, I think,' he drawled.

Erin's eyes flashed. 'How dare you criticise my mother?'

'You are angry because you know I am right,' he observed with unforgivable accuracy. 'However, I did not come here to discuss your mother.' *I came here to hear you tell me you are carrying my child.* 'There are things we need to discuss.'

As Erin met his dark eyes her secret had never felt more of a burden. She gave an indifferent sniff.

'You're miserable?' He looked as though the idea did not displease him. 'Well, if you are it's your own doing. You are the author of your own misery, Erin.' *And mine.*

The claim made her stare. *'Me...!'* She loosed an incredulous laugh.

He bared his teeth in a white humourless smile. 'Yes, you!' he flung back, dragging a shapely hand through his dark hair. 'From the outset you did not trust me. Every absence you expected me to account for, every woman I spoke to you regarded with suspicion.' Breathing hard, Francesco fought to contain his escalating resentment and anger.

'You weren't talking to that woman, you were kissing her!' The knife-cut of jealousy and betrayal was just as painful now as it had been on that night.

'Erin, she had been drinking champagne—she kissed me.'

His dismissive shrug made Erin see red. Breathing hard, she pinned him with an angry glare. She doubted he would dismiss it so readily if the situation had been reversed!

Of course he'd managed to make the entire situation seem perfectly innocent, but how many times had she seen her father offer a totally plausible explanation for his serial philandering? He had been so convincing that half the time her mother had ended up apologising for doubting him! She was never ever going to fall into that trap.

'So you're the innocent victim?' she suggested bitterly.

Francesco dragged an angry hand through his hair. 'What was I meant to do...scream?' he suggested derisively. 'Have her arrested? Tell her my wife will think we're in love?'

His biting sarcasm brought a fresh flush of anger to her cheeks. 'What you were not meant to do was kiss her back,' she retorted.

'Grow up, Erin!'

The weary recommendation drew a sharp gasp of anger from her throat.

'And don't blame me for your self-esteem issues.'

'Don't try and make it out to be about *my* problem.'

But didn't he have a point? Hadn't part of the problem been that deep down she had never really been able to believe that a man like Francesco could really want somebody like her? She had turned a deaf ear to her doubts because she had wanted him so much, but had she ever really expected it to last?

Francesco's dark lashes lifted from his chiselled cheek-bones that were lent extra prominence at that moment by the two bands of febrile colour along the sharp angles. His eyes were smouldering with an anger he was barely suppressing. 'You haven't the faintest idea what is typical of me, Erin, or you would not treat me this way.'

'Is that a threat?'

He folded his arms across his chest and gave a slow, dangerous smile that made her heart beat a little faster. 'It is a simple statement of fact—'

The response dragged a dry laugh that bordered on hysteria from her aching throat…nothing about Francesco was *simple*. Her life had become impossibly complicated from the moment they had met!

Every time he looked at her the sheer enormity of her betrayal in concealing her pregnancy hit Francesco afresh.

Part of him wanted to demand the truth from her. He might have done just that had the situation not been further complicated by the fact he couldn't look at her without experiencing an even *stronger* compulsion to pull her into his arms and fill his nostrils with her warm feminine scent.

His bleak eyes stilled on her angry face. 'What happened to the woman I married?'

The unexpected question sent a stab of pain through Erin. The expression in his eyes told her that whatever feelings he had had for the woman he spoke of were dead. The realisation hurt a lot more than it ought to have.

'The woman who was warm and spontaneous…'

Erin tossed her head and shrugged. The weak quiver in her voice spoiled her tough pose as she claimed belligerently, 'She w-wised up.'

'Your father cheats therefore all men cheat?'

Erin's eyes fell from his uncomfortably perceptive gaze. Francesco had touched on a subject that had been in her thoughts frequently during the last few weeks, and common sense told her he had a point.

A person couldn't watch her mother choose time after time to believe her cheating husband's lies rather than face the truth and not be affected in some way. Had she been so determined not to allow herself to become a victim whom people pitied that she had made a terrible mistake? For as long as she could remember she'd despised her mother for believing the lies her father told. *Am I so damned sure,* she asked herself, *that I won't do exactly what Mum did?*

She couldn't let herself find out.

Not that the question was anything but academic now; she had made her decision and there was no going back even if she had wanted to.

'Sometimes, Erin,' she heard him say as she passed a not quite steady hand across her eyes, 'an innocent kiss is just that, innocent. Your reaction was totally irrational; you must realise that.'

Erin shook her head in stubborn rejection. 'I don't consider it *irrational* to expect fidelity.'

'*You* were the woman I married.' *The woman who is carrying my child.* He dragged his eyes upwards from her still-flat stomach where they kept drifting.

His original intention had been to confront Erin immediately. His plan had been simple: reveal the phone, play back the message and watch her face when she realised that he knew her secret.

Now he found himself wondering how long she would be prepared to prolong this lie of omission. How long she would be able to look him in the eye and conceal the truth.

'*You* were the woman I wanted to spend the rest of my life with...'

The throaty catch in his deep voice brought Erin's downcast eyes sweeping upwards. It wasn't the molten anger she encountered as their eyes connected that drew the involuntary gasp of shock from her throat, but the unexpected glitter of pain and loss she saw in the smoky, expressive depths of his thickly lashed eyes.

'That,' he added, bracing one hand against the back of a leather armchair, 'should have been enough for you.'

A full thirty seconds' nerve-shredding silence elapsed before Erin could drag her eyes from his mesmeric dark gaze. 'You mean I should take whatever crumbs you throw in my direction and not ask too many awkward questions.'

'I mean that my word should have been enough for you.'

'I should have been enough for you,' she countered, dismayed because his simple statement increased her growing sense of irrational guilt.

But was it irrational? What if it was merited? A chill swept over her at the unbidden thought and without wanting to she remembered how none of the many who had witnessed the embrace on the night of the ball had looked at her with anything that approached discomfort when Francesco had ruefully disentangled himself from the tipsy blonde.

I'm not the one who had cause to feel guilty, she reminded herself deliberately. The image of the curvaceous blonde plastered all over him brought the taste of bile to Erin's mouth.

They had been married almost a month and had still been enjoying their extended honeymoon. The charity ball in Venice, a glittering society affair, had been the first—and as it turned out the last—public event they had attended together.

It was his intention, Francesco had explained, to use the occasion to show off his beautiful new wife to the world.

It had clearly not occurred to him that the idea of being paraded in public scared her stiff.

When he had commented with some concern on her quietness the day leading up to the ball, Erin had finally confessed that she was nervous.

'What if I let you down by using the wrong fork or saying the wrong thing? What if your friends don't like me?'

Francesco seemed astonished by her anxieties, but she had already worked out that concern for what people thought of him did not register with the man she had married.

He laughed at her fears. 'Of course they'll like you. Just be yourself.'

'I will,' she promised, wishing that *herself* was more interesting.

So dressed in unaccustomed designer finery, her confidence buoyed by the sensual glow in Francesco's eyes as she had paraded before him in the slim black silk sheath dress that swished deliciously against her bare legs as she moved, Erin walked in beside her handsome husband. Her head held high, her stomach tied in nervous knots.

The scene inside the spectacular room took her breath away. She was dazzled as much by the people as the chandeliers glittering overhead.

The first people Francesco introduced her to were a colleague of his, and his wife.

The sophisticated-looking brunette was so charming to her that Erin actually began to relax and think that this might not be so bad after all. This made her even less prepared for the sudden change in the older woman's manner when the men briefly excused themselves to speak to a mutual acquaintance.

Her charming smile stayed fixed, but there was a hostility in the other woman's eyes that bordered on malice as she looked Erin up and down in a way that brought Erin's insecurities rushing back.

'Married? Well, you've succeeded where many before you have failed, so I suppose there must be something more to you than meets the eye. I can't say I envy you…Francesco is the sort of man who makes a perfect lover, and I'm not the only woman in the room tonight who is in a position to vouch for that. But as a husband?' She arched an artfully shaped brow. 'He would, I think, be difficult to manage.'

The men returned before Erin could respond and the woman switched to being sweetness and light again, going as far as to suggest that Erin join her for lunch the following week.

Erin smiled and thought, *Over my dead body*.

Francesco, one hand lightly in the small of her back, bent his head to speak in her ear as they left the other couple. 'See—I told you everyone would love you.'

Shivering in response to the warmth of his breath on her neck, she lifted her head and smiled serenely. 'So you did, but you're prejudiced…at least,' she amended, 'I hope you are?'

Deep down she had never been able to believe that a man like her lethally handsome husband could really be satisfied with someone as ordinary as her and the evil seeds of distrust the other woman had planted in Erin's mind fed on this self doubt.

Of course, she accepted that there must have been other women in Francesco's life—her husband was a very sensual, passionate man. But after the brunette's malicious comments Erin found it hard not to wonder when she saw a beautiful woman look at Francesco—was there some secret message in her smile?

When she found herself on the brink of asking a particularly lovely woman if she had ever been Francesco's lover Erin knew she had let things get out of hand. She excused herself and took refuge in the ladies' room.

It was unfortunate that when she emerged a short while later almost able to laugh at her paranoia, the first thing she saw was her husband locked in a passionate embrace with a tall, leggy blonde.

As Francesco came up for air, his dark, sleek hair dishevelled from the clinch, his eyes met Erin's over the woman's shoulder. If he had displayed some sort of remorse or guilt that would have been something, but instead he rolled his eyes and gave a wry grin as if inviting her to share the joke. The humour died from his face to be replaced by concern and puzzlement as he saw Erin's expression.

As he bodily put the tipsy blonde away from him and took a step towards her Erin gathered her long skirts in one hand and fled, not caring about the startled and speculative looks her exit drew.

Francesco caught up with her outside.

His initial concern quickly turned to annoyance when she rashly accused him of humiliating her.

'Do not be ridiculous,' he recommended curtly. 'Diane is totally harmless. She has just had a little too much to drink. If I wanted to embark on an illicit affair I would hardly advertise the fact to five hundred people who know me.'

'Have you ever slept with her?' The moment the words were out of her mouth she regretted them, but it was too late. Francesco's expression had frozen into one of icy displeasure.

'What I did before we were married is none of your business.'

'But what you do after is.'

'I am not your father, Erin.'

The soft words stopped Erin in her tracks. 'This has nothing whatever to do with my parents' marriage.'

He angled a dark brow. 'You're not stupid; I don't think you really believe that.'

Erin shook her head. 'I want to leave,' she said, flinching away when he touched her shoulder.

Francesco looked down at her, disdain and anger etched on his patrician features. 'We will not leave yet.'

'You can do what the hell you like!' she yelled back. 'I'm leaving. You stay; I'm sure you won't be lonely.'

'*Dio!*' he breathed. Eyes narrowed, he stood there, the angles and planes of his face thrown into sharp relief by the lights illuminating the tree behind him.

'You seem determined to push me into another woman's arms,' he observed in a voice that seemed clean of all emotion. 'Be careful, Erin—you just might get your wish,' he warned before turning and striding towards the façade of the brightly illuminated building without a backward glance.

CHAPTER EIGHT

ERIN physically shaking in reaction to the row, had hailed a cab and returned to their hotel suite; by this time doubts about the moral high ground she had claimed had crept in. Her self-righteous anger had been the only thing holding back the tears and when that had dissipated the floodgates had opened and she had flung herself on the bed and wept.

Examining her tear-stained face in the mirror when the storm had subsided, she had forced herself to look at the evening's events through Francesco's eyes.

It had not made pleasant viewing!

'You've got a problem,' she told her reflection.

Still, problems had solutions, and Erin gave the matter a lot of serious thought as she stood under the reviving spray of the shower.

She decided that she had to be totally open and frank with Francesco. She genuinely thought that they could work this through together...she just hoped that after tonight he still thought their marriage was worth the effort!

Despite all her protests it was pretty hard under the circumstances to continue to claim that her parents' dysfunctional marriage had not left its mark. When it came to men she had some serious trust issues.

It wasn't that she actually believed deep down that Francesco had any intention of being unfaithful. Her aggressive overreaction that evening had more to do with her deep-seated and previously unacknowledged fear that if faced with a similar situation she would react as her mother had.

Erin awaited his return with a mixture of trepidation and resolution. She would not give up on this marriage. It was the best thing that had ever happened to her.

Francesco was the best thing that had ever happened to her!

By three-thirty she was feeling less upbeat.

Around six-thirty she finally realised Francesco wasn't coming back at all. Her soul-searching of the night before now seemed utterly pathetic. While she had been trying to think of ways to heal their marriage he had been hitting out at her by sleeping with the first warm and willing body.

Recalling his warning parting shot, she didn't know why it had taken her this long to work that one out.

Erin knew without soul-searching that the one thing that was a total deal-breaker for her was infidelity—she couldn't and *wouldn't* live with that!

Around eight-thirty, looking more piratical than ever with the dark shadow on his lower face lending him an air of dangerously attractive dissipation, Francesco finally returned.

'What are you doing?' he asked, propping his shoulders against the wall.

She zipped up her flight bag and straightened up. Reminding herself of the reason for his drained and exhausted appearance enabled her to treat him to a dazzling and icy smile of total indifference.

'I'm doing exactly what it looks like. Now, if you'll excuse me—I'll be late for my flight.'

The colour seeped out from under his tan. He appeared genuinely shocked by her attitude. 'You're not serious?'

'Never more so,' she promised, fighting the crazy compulsion she had to sweep the hank of dark hair from his brow.

'We need to talk about this.'

'Why? Are you going to tell there's a perfectly innocent reason for you staying out all night?'

He shook his head. 'No, it doesn't work that way. You either trust me or you don't.' He gave a take-it-or-leave-it shrug that made her want to scream in sheer frustration. 'What you believe is up to you. Your problem, Erin, is as much as you despise me at the moment you despise yourself more...because you want me anyway. And that,' he concluded with terrifying accuracy, 'is tearing you up inside.'

It was as if he had been walking around inside her head. The idea was not a comfortable one. 'Who says I want you?'

His eyes, dark and cynical, locked on to hers. 'You don't really need me to answer that, do you?'

The mortified heat flew to her cheeks.

'This is a waste of time. There is nothing to talk about—you made your choice last night.'

She liked to think that if he had tried to stop her she would have had the resolution to walk away. But she'd never know because he didn't try, he just stood there and let her leave.

'You rejected me.'

The sound of his deep voice dragged Erin's wandering thoughts back to the present with a jolt. *Reject*...was that how he saw it? She was astonished at this interpretation.

He took a step closer.

'What have you been doing to yourself, Erin?' He looked at her parchment-pale face and something twisted in his chest.

He might no longer believe himself to be in love, but this was the mother of his child; it was only natural that he should feel a strong desire to protect her.

'You are nothing but skin and bone!' he condemned, frowning at the sharp angles of her delicate collar-bones as he reached into his jacket pocket and pulled out his hand a moment later empty. Was it so unreasonable of him to want her to tell him about the baby of her own volition?

She lifted her eyes to his. If ever a moment screamed perfect, this was it. *Tell him*, said the voice in her head. *Tell him...!*

She sucked in a deep steadying breath. 'I'm...the thing is, Francesco, I'm...' Hit without warning by a sudden wave of dizziness, she swayed and lifted a hand to her head as the colour drained from her face.

'Shall I call a doctor?'

'No, I'm fine.'

Her head was pressed to his chest, the hand that cradled her skull was holding it there next to his heart. Having lost the last twenty seconds, she had no idea how she came to be in this position. She just knew that the moment had passed.

Being this close to him was agony.

Erin felt his long fingers slide through her hair and...a choking sound escaped her clamped lips.

'Clearly you are not.' Francesco tilted her face up to his. She was looking at him with a suppressed longing she could not in that moment conceal. His expression abstracted, his finger traced the soft curve of her jaw.

'There are shadows under your eyes.' The discovery of the violet smudges made him frown and mutter something she didn't understand in his native tongue.

'Really, I'm fine.'

'You nearly fainted. That is not "fine." *Dio,* but I find English stoicism irritating.'

Erin took a deep breath and, hands pressed to his chest, pushed hard. His hands remained curved around her upper arms preventing her stepping back.

'Not just English stoicism,' she muttered.

One corner of his mobile mouth twitched into a half-smile as their eyes met. 'No, you I find infuriating.'

On the brink of smiling back, Erin stopped herself and frowned. 'I'm not ill, Francesco.' Pregnancy was not an illness, though this was hard to remember some mornings!

He angled a sardonic brow and let her go. 'You make a habit of fainting?'

'I did not faint.' Though the past few weeks there had been a few close calls, but the doctor had soothed her concerns and told her that this was normal, especially as her blood pressure was unusually low. 'I just…lost my balance for a moment. And you have no rights, Francesco, not where I'm concerned anyhow.'

But he had rights where his child was concerned. She pressed a hand to her stomach and wondered how many of those rights he would avail himself of.

God, I have to tell him.

She looked at him and thought, *I can't do it! I need to psych myself up…I need to find the right words.* In the back of her mind Erin knew that there were no magical right words. She knew she was only delaying the inevitable.

'Don't you think it might be an idea to sit down just in case you *lose your balance* again?'

'What? Yes, fine.' She tore her eyes from the muscle that was clenching in his shadowed jaw and sat down in the nearest armchair.

'I'm still waiting to hear why you've come here, Francesco.'

'I came here hoping that you might have stopped avoiding issues.'

If only you knew the half of it!

She opened her mouth, but the words wouldn't come. Her shaking fingers massaging the skin of her throbbing temples, she shook her head in a negative gesture.

A hiss of frustration escaped Francesco's lips. 'Marriage is not something you throw away casually.'

'I'm not doing anything casually.'

'Walking out the way you did was hardly something you put a lot of thought into, was it?' he retorted.

'Well, the situation seems to have suited you.'

'You base that statement on what exactly?' The furrow in his brow deepened as he mused. 'Or was it an accusation?' he speculated.

'Well, until you got my letter you seemed happy with the situation.' Erin's stomach lurched sickly as her eyes fell from his. It would be too much to hope he hadn't heard the quivering note of bitterness in her voice.

'You expected me to run after you?'

She started to shake her head in denial while he was still speaking.

A slow smile crossed his lean features. 'You *wanted* me to chase after you.' He sounded smug about the discovery.

'That's the *last* thing I wanted,' she denied, her cheeks burning with mortification at the suggestion. 'I was relieved that when you thought about it, you realised I was right.'

'Now whatever gave you that idea, *cara*?'

Her head lifted. 'Because you're not a passive person. If you'd wanted me…' She stopped, hot, mortified colour flooding her face. 'You're not the sort of man who would meekly stand to one side and let something happen if it's not what you actually want.'

'So what you're saying is I don't want you, *cara*.'

'Don't call me that!' she spat, covering her ears with her hands.

'Cue a ranting irrational outburst. Now that,' he mused, sounding bored, 'was predictable.'

'What was? What are you looking at me like that for?'

'Whenever you get close to acknowledging a problem you start an argument to deflect the discussion…either that or,' he observed with a hard laugh, 'you pack your bags.'

Her denial was automatic. 'That's ridiculous.'

Francesco's brows lifted. 'Is it?' he asked, dragging a hand through his dark hair. 'I think if you let your mind drift back…'

Did he have a point? Her expression troubled, Erin shook her head in rejection of his theory. 'How is this suddenly my problem, my fault? You spent the night with another woman.'

Still scanning her flushed face, he shook his head. 'I don't think that deep down even *you* are insecure enough to believe that. No, infidelity wasn't the problem in our marriage.'

She folded her arms across her chest and tried to disguise the fact his assessment of the situation had shaken her deeply, and raised some uncomfortable questions in her mind.

'So you're saying I was the problem? Even if I was wrong,' she said, grudgingly conceding to herself for the first time that it was possible, 'it was only a matter of time before you did cheat.'

There was a moment's silence.

'Now that was a very revealing comment. Don't you think so, *cara*?'

Hating the feeling of exposure, of emotional vulnerability, Erin shook her head mutely.

'So you left in anticipation of my cheating on you just as your father cheated on your mother.'

'This isn't about my parents!'

'I know that, but do you? Let me be clear, Erin. What you are basically saying is that you never expected me to be faithful. You never expected our marriage to last. Does the term self-fulfilling prophesy mean anything to you?'

'You've been telling me half-truths from the moment you met me.' She heard the defensive note in her voice and bit her lip.

He hit her with his trump card then and watched the guilt wash over her face. 'And your conscience is totally clear on the truth, whole truth and nothing but the truth front, is it?' He watched the stricken look of guilt spread across her face and was surprised to find it did not afford him the satisfaction he had anticipated.

Erin studied the toe of her shoe with deep interest as she tried to force the words from her dry throat. 'Francesco, I'm…'

'You're pregnant.'

Her head came up with a jerk. Her wide, shocked eyes meshed with his implacable dark, accusing stare. The air between them vibrated with a static electricity that was almost visible.

'What did you say?' Her lips moved, but did the words come out? Erin wasn't sure—the blood was pounding so hard in her ears that it drowned out everything else. She gave her head a tiny shake to clear her confused, chaotic thoughts… How could he know?

'You heard me, Erin: *pregnant.* You are with child…*my* child.' His voice dropped a note with each addition and every syllable contained the same fury that was etched in the strong bones of his lean, patrician face.

She shook her head in bewilderment. 'I don't understand…how?'

'How?' Francesco echoed, in a thickly accented voice that was so hard she barely recognised it. 'This is how.'

Erin stared blankly at the mobile phone he flung onto the chair. 'I don't understand.'

'The hospital left a message concerning your antenatal appointment.'

Still wearing a shell-shocked expression, she picked up the phone. 'I must have given my old number. You really shouldn't have been listening to my private messages, Francesco.' She realised even before Francesco swore forcibly in his own tongue that it had been a stupid thing to say.

'I do apologise for violating your privacy,' he drawled, sounding anything but and looking… Her eyes skimmed his face and her heart dropped like a stone—*angry* didn't really cover the explosive fury that was oozing from every perfect, rampantly male pore. Francesco was incandescent!

'However, I think, *cara*, that my *transgression* pales into insignificance compared to your own. I did not try and rob you of your child, Erin.'

Horrified by his interpretation, she lifted her face in shaky protest. 'That wasn't what I was doing! I was going to tell you. I *really* was…'

There was no softening in his harsh, condemnatory attitude as she spread her hands towards him in a gesture of appeal. If anything it seemed to Erin that her silent entreaty had fed the flames of his fury.

He angled a dark brow sardonically and wondered with

blighting sarcasm, 'When exactly? Or were you going to send me an e-mail after you gave birth?'

'Does it matter?' Erin's shoulders slumped, because clearly what she said didn't matter. Nothing she said or did was ever going to excuse her silence in Francesco's eyes.

'It matters to *me*, it matters to me that my wife thought it unnecessary to inform me she is carrying my child. It matters to me that she has deliberately tried to conceal her condition from me, though,' he added, shaking his dark head slowly from side to side, 'how you thought that was going to work I can't even begin to imagine. You seem to have lost your grip on reality. What were you planning to do—change your name and flee the country?'

Face screwed up in anguish, she shook her head violently from side to side. 'You make it sound as though I was deliberately trying to deceive you!' she protested.

'And you weren't?'

Erin literally wrung her hands as she struggled to convince him of her sincerity. 'I can see how it might seem that way to you, but, no—no, it wasn't like that at all.'

Francesco's hands clenched at his sides as he steeled himself to ignore the anguish in her tear-filled blue eyes. 'What was it *like*, Erin? Shall I tell you what it was *like* for me? What it was like to pick up that phone and hear some anonymous voice talk about antenatal appointments?'

'I know,' she sighed, 'and I wouldn't have had that happen for the world, but it's just complicated things… I know that sounds pathetic.'

He didn't disagree, just carried on looking at her with simmering hostility.

'I knew I had to tell you at some point, but, well…using a child to paper over cracks in a marriage is never a good idea.

And I was afraid that you might have a knee-jerk reaction and…suggest that we had to stay together for the sake of the baby.' Sweeping a tangled skein of bright glossy hair back from her face, she angled a wary gaze at Francesco. He was listening to her and, much to her relief, seemed more in control of his feelings. But the expression in his hooded eyes was frustratingly hard to read.

'Which is clearly ridiculous?' Her voice lifted in query as she tried to gauge his reaction. Maybe her fears were misplaced?

It would be ironic considering how much she'd stressed about the possibility if it didn't even occur to Francesco to suggest they give their marriage another shot for the sake of the baby. After all, he might be a man with some surprisingly old-fashioned ideas about family, but Francesco was also a realist.

'Ridiculous to want to salvage our marriage to provide a home and stability for our child?'

Their eyes connected and she realised that she had been right to stress—in fact it seemed likely she had not stressed enough. 'You mean pretend…'

From the way he was looking at her at that moment Erin imagined that Francesco would struggle to maintain a pretence that the sight of her didn't make him feel physically ill let alone spend their married life acting as though she were the love of his life!

'That's hardly realistic, is it, Francesco?'

'Not as unrealistic as you imagining I will give you a quickie divorce!' he retorted bluntly.

'Well, there is no point in hanging around, really, is there? I know some people stay separated for years before they make it official, but—'

'There will be no separation.'

The interruption made her pause. 'I don't understand.'

'Then let me spell it out for you.' His silky smile was somehow infinitely more alarming than his raging anger had been. Now he was in control. A shiver of apprehension traced its way down Erin's spine. 'No separation, no divorce, not now, not ever!'

'What do you mean?' she asked in a small voice, even though his statement had been clear enough. This was her worst nightmare coming true.

'You wish me to spell it out? My child will not be brought up not knowing his father, his family, not speaking his own language.'

Erin rushed to reassure him that this had never been her intention. 'Look, of course he'll learn about his heritage—there was never any question of—'

'You will come back to Italy with me where our child will be born.'

Erin shook her head in a negative gesture at the casually autocratic decree. 'You're suggesting that for the sake of the baby…'

'I'm not *suggesting* anything,' he corrected. 'This is not a discussion. I'm telling you what is going to happen.'

Erin tried to laugh, but all that emerged was a high-pitched squeaky sound. 'You can't force me…' The reminder was as much for her own benefit as his.

'I'm sure that won't be necessary—not once you have considered the options.'

'What options?'

Again he smiled and the hairs on the nape of her neck stood on end. 'There are none.'

She struggled to inject some sanity into the conversation. 'You're not being reasonable, Francesco. Our marriage was a total disaster. We can't stay married just because of the baby.'

His jaw tightened. 'Perhaps you need reminding why you married me in the first instance.'

Her head came up with a jerk. As their eyes clashed there was a tension in the air that reminded Erin of the heavy heat that preceded a storm.

'Come to bed with me.'

The colour flew to her parchment-pale cheeks. 'You're so manipulative! You think that you can make me agree to anything if you get me in bed, don't you?' Why wouldn't he? So far it had worked pretty well!

'Manipulation? You actually imagine that I am capable of such clarity of thought with you in the same room?'

Erin blinked, confused by the emotions that were rolling off him in waves.

'I invite you into my bed because it is where you belong.'

The blunt pronouncement made her stomach dip and flutter.

'I find it hard to function when all I can think about is sinking into you.'

For a moment their eyes clung. The raw need in his drove the air from her lungs. From some hidden well of reserve she discovered the strength to break that searing contact.

With a cry she ran from the room, not caring if her flight confirmed his accusation that she was too immature to confront her feelings.

CHAPTER NINE

ERIN went straight to her room. It took her less than five minutes to pack her bags, throwing things in a blind panic. She didn't see another person in the apparently deserted house until she had reached the hallway.

'Isn't this becoming a habit with you, *cara*?'

Erin dropped her case as she spun around in time to see a tall, lithe figure peel away from the wall.

'There is a problem you don't want to confront. So you run away.'

'I'm not running away.'

'No?' He arched a brow. 'What are you doing, then?'

Erin drew a deep startled breath and stiffened when without warning his long brown fingers brushed her skin as they slid into the neckline of her shirt.

The contact sizzled like a flame fizzing along her nerve endings all the way down to her curling toes. She closed her eyes, her nostrils flaring in response to the male scent of his warm body so close now that all she had to do was lean forward and their bodies would be touching.

She wanted that contact so much that it was a physical pain. She wanted to feel his hands on her, his mouth…

She had begun to sway towards him when she heard him say. 'Why do you wear this?'

Her eyelids felt heavy as she forced her eyes open and, blinking in a bemused fashion, she focused on his lean dark face so close to her own that she could see the fine mesh of lines that radiated from the corners of his incredible eyes. 'What? I…'

Then she saw it.

The gold ring still warm from her skin resting in the palm of his cupped hand. The heat of arousal drained from her body.

Francesco's expression was inscrutable as he stared at the circlet of gold on his palm, still warm from its hiding place in the valley between her breasts.

His eyes darkened and a muscle alongside his sensually sculpted mouth clenched as he recalled how perfectly her breast fitted into that same palm.

'Why did you not throw it away? Surely it represents a memory that can give you no pleasure?'

Francesco did not attempt to stop her as she snatched the ring from his hand and drew back a clenched fist pressed to her chest. Her angry eyes held his defiantly as she allowed it to slide back into its hiding place between her breasts and then fastened the top two buttons of her blouse.

'I keep it as a reminder, just in case the unthinkable happens and I suffer another bout of temporary insanity and even *consider* getting married again.'

'You *are* married.'

Her eyes dropped from the anger in his. 'I need time to think, Francesco.'

'There is nothing to think about—a child needs two parents.'

As she moved towards the door so did Francesco, his intention obviously to cut her off. She might have reached it before him if the strap of the bag she had looped around her neck hadn't got caught up on a heavy ormolu clock that took pride of place on a console table.

As she was pulled backwards, half strangled by the strap around her neck, her elbow caught a large vase filled with water and before it shattered noisily it managed to tip its contents all over Francesco.

It was the look of shock on his face as he stood there with water dripping from his drenched shirt and trousers onto the floor that drew the laugh from Erin's throat and once she had started she couldn't stop. The laughter gradually morphed into sobs, tears ran unchecked down her cheeks as the deep racking sobs; shook her entire body.

'*Per amor di Dio!*' Francesco groaned, his face contorted as though in pain as he watched her.

Erin did not resist as he gently removed the leather strap from her neck, but when he tried to drag her into his arms she shook her head and pulled back, wiping the tears from her face with the back of her hand.

'You're right. I was running away.' She realised that Francesco had been right about a lot of things.

'That is understandable under the circumstances,' he observed.

Erin was inclined to view his sudden tolerance with suspicion. Her eyes lifted, and for a moment the sheer sensational beauty of Francesco's face took her breath away. It wasn't just the perfect symmetry he had been blessed with, but the intelligence, authority and sensuality stamped on his features that made him totally devastating.

His dark eyes dropped, his thick lashes casting dark shadows across his cheekbones as he placed a hand on her belly. She could feel the warmth of his strong fingers through the thin layers of clothing.

'There is a growing life inside you, Erin.'

Her throat aching with the emotional tears locked there, she nodded.

'A life we made. You will be a good mother.'

'I hope so.' *One word of praise from him and I'm glowing… Oh, God*, she thought despairingly, *I'm hopeless.*

'You would give your life for our child.' His fingers tightened fractionally across her abdomen.

'Of course,' she said, feeling ridiculously bereft when he lifted his hand.

'But living with me is too great a sacrifice?'

'I'd do anything that I think would be in the baby's best interests, but I don't think us staying married would be.' She stopped and croaked in panic, 'What are you doing?'

Francesco continued to unbutton his soiled shirt before shrugging it off.

Erin tried not to stare.

It wasn't easy. There was a lot to stare at and all of it perfect.

There wasn't an ounce of surplus flesh on his lean, sleek body. The golden skin of his bronzed torso gleamed under a layer of sweat that delineated each individual slab of perfectly formed muscle.

Desire like a tight fist clutched at the muscles low in her belly as her gaze slid helplessly down the long, lean length of his body and things dissolved inside her.

The corners of his mouth curled sardonically as he unzipped his trousers. 'I would have thought that was fairly self-explanatory.'

Erin looked into his eyes and fought the breathless drowning sensation that threatened to overwhelm her. She closed her eyes as he stepped out of his shoes and ruined trousers.

'You can't do that. What if someone sees you?'

'There is no one here but you and me. Our hosts have made sure that the house is empty...' His dark eyes held an unmistakable message as they captured hers.

Erin's nerve endings tingled as desire slammed through her body with a force that expelled the air from her lungs in a raw, fractured gasp. Her lashes came down in a concealing curtain, but not before he'd seen her pupils dilate.

'You can't leave those things there,' she grunted, touching his discarded clothes with the toe of her shoe. She leapt like a startled deer as his hand came up to frame one side of her face.

After a few moments of standing there motionless, tension and his light touch the only thing keeping her upright, Erin gritted her teeth and closed her eyes.

With a muttered, 'Idiot,' she turned her face sharply to one side; his hand immediately fell away. Even though it was no longer there she could feel the imprint of his fingers like a brand on her skin. She bit down hard on her full lower lip as she fought an overwhelming compulsion to reach for his hand and place it back on her face.

She had to be strong.

For a long moment he studied her face, his expression enigmatic.

'I did not cheat.'

The abrupt statement made her turn her head away. His comment about 'self-fulfilling prophecy' came back to her. The truth was she was half inclined to believe him even though she didn't want to; the world was already shifting under her feet in a very uncomfortable way.

If she believed him, then by implication she accepted that he'd been right when he'd said she was the author of her own misery.

She shook her head in denial. 'As one with some experience on the subject, I have to tell you that showing a little humility and coming clean generally has better results than a flat denial.'

'I think your "experience on the subject" is what is distorting your view. And before you ask, no, I can't prove it to you—I can't prove I spent the night walking…' He stopped and shook his head. 'No, what I did and where I went is not the point. The point is that I shouldn't have to prove it. Why should you assume that you're the only one to consider a wedding ring guaranteed exclusivity?'

The silence stretched.

Some of the anger faded from Francesco's face as he looked at her downbent head. 'When I made my vows I meant them.'

In the middle of a loud sniff her head came up with a jerky motion. His use of tense was not lost on her.

'This is ridiculous. You will listen to me, Erin…that night I—'

Realising his intention, she shook her head. 'I don't want to hear it and I'm not coming back to Italy with you.' She pressed a hand to her stomach in a fruitless attempt to ease the aching, empty sensation deep down. 'The truth is, together we don't work. We're just incompatible. I'm ready to concede that it's partly my fault, but I am who I am, Francesco—I can't change that.'

Francesco closed his eyes and snarled an oath under his breath. He pushed back his anger and let his eyes fall away from her earnest stare. His glance fell as far as the heaving contours of her small, perfect breasts and stopped dead.

He knew they were perfect not because the top was suggestively skimpy, but because he had cupped them in his hands, kneaded the warm, firm flesh and aroused the tight pink nipples with his fingers and tongue.

In his head he could hear her hoarse cry of pleasure as she speared her fingers into his hair, holding him close as her body arched with pleasure.

She had been the most exquisitely sensitive creature; even the sound of his voice could draw the most incredible response from her. *Still is sensitive*…said the voice in his head.

In his mind he visualised the frustration building up in him as a wall, a crumbling wall with several gaping holes in it.

Breathing harder than he did during a strenuous workout he turned to pick up his clothes from the floor, presenting his back to her. The breathing space afforded him an opportunity to regain some degree of control over the compelling over-powering urge he had to slide his hand under that top and stroke the warm silky skin it covered.

Erin, who had been staring at the smooth, graceful lines of his strong, golden-skinned back with longing, blushed guiltily when he straightened up and looked at her. His lashes skimmed the hard angle of his cheekbones as his darkened glance dropped to her mouth and stayed there.

Erin's own lashes came down in a dark silky screen. 'Do you understand what I'm saying?' she said severely.

'There are some levels at which we work very well, Erin.'

She gave a shrug that was meant to convey supreme indif-ference to the honeyed implication, but spoilt the effect by being unable to hold his gaze.

'This blushing *ingénue* act is a little misplaced when you're talking to a man who has an intimate knowledge of your body.'

Erin's head lifted with a jerk. 'If you think I find your ar-rogance arousing…' she gritted her teeth and felt the heat fly to her cheeks '…and if you think you can embarrass me, Francesco…' The wolfish grin that spread across his lean face made her voice dry.

'Oh, I *know* I can do that, *mia bella*.' Their eyes locked and his dangerous smile faded, leaving an intense burning look that was infinitely more dangerous. It was also exciting, but Erin refused to acknowledge this even to herself.

'What are you doing, Francesco?' she asked, trying to sound calm and practical and feeling neither as he began to walk slowly but with purpose towards her.

Framing her face in one big hand, he smiled. It was a smile that stripped away the thin veneer of urbane charm he presented to the world. When she looked into his midnight eyes Erin saw the raw, untamed, masculine heart of him.

Her pulses leapt in wild response to the primitive need stamped into every angle and plane of his strong, heartbreakingly beautiful face.

He wanted her, but not in the same way she wanted him; he wasn't capable of that. She knew there could only ever be sex between them, but the emotions that ached in her throat didn't understand the distinction.

The fear and fascination she felt was mirrored in her eyes as she looked through her lashes at his face.

His thumb moved gently over the curve of her cheek and her eyelids fluttered briefly. It was a light butterfly caress, but more than enough to vaporise every instinct for self-preservation she possessed.

'I'm doing this, *cara mia*,' he explained in a voice as thick and rich as warm honey. His burning dark eyes roamed over her face, examining every inch of the smooth, peachy pale skin with a hungry intensity, as though he was committing each individual freckle, every soft hollow and curve to memory.

Erin's throat ached and her heart thudded against her breastbone as, light-headed with anticipation, she waited to feel his mouth on hers. She was sure that if Francesco didn't kiss her soon she would become the first documented case of someone dying from *not* being kissed.

A whimper of relief caught in her throat when he did finally bend his dark head and fit his mouth to hers. It was as if she had been waiting a lifetime for this to happen. He kissed her slowly, tasting her, deepening the kiss as her lips parted under the seductive pressure and friction of his mouth.

With a lost sigh Erin slid her slim arms around his neck and leaned into him. She met the stabbing incursions of his tongue with her own, moaning into his mouth and tangling her fingers into the heavy silky strands of his dark hair.

When he lifted her into his arms she did not resist but moaned softly into his mouth. She lay curled up in his arms, her hands linked around his neck, her fingers trailing into the hair on his nape as he strode swiftly down the hallway to a room at the far end and kicked open the door with his foot.

Once inside he walked purposefully over to the large four-poster bed and laying her on it, came to kneel beside her.

The tightness in her chest increased as her hungry gaze roamed over his smooth golden skin. The blood pounded in her ears as she looked at him; he was so beautiful it hurt.

'This is probably not a good idea,' she observed in a tone that invited—no, *begged* for—denial.

'Do you care?'

Her eyes lifted to his face.

Francesco's dark, restless glance repeatedly drifted towards her mouth as though drawn by invisible forces to the soft, full, quivering outline.

'Well, do you?' he challenged throatily.

Slowly she shook her head.

A sigh that seemed to Erin's fanciful imagination to be drawn from his soul shuddered through Francesco's lean frame.

'I should, though…' The faint addition was as much for her own benefit as his.

He dismissed her words with an expressive shrug. 'If we both did what we should life would be very predictable.'

'But safe.' At that moment it was hard for Erin to remember what safe had felt like.

He responded to her husky claim by planting a hand either side of her head and kissing her hard, silenced her protest with deep, penetrating stabs of his tongue that made her stomach dissolve.

'*Dio mio,*' he panted against her mouth. 'I want this…I want you…I want to feel your hands on my skin.'

'Like this?' she suggested. Laying one hand palm-flat on his stomach, she felt the muscles under the silky hair-roughened surface immediately contract and quiver as she stroked his damp skin.

Francesco sucked in a harsh breath. His eyes glittered as though lit from within as he slid his warm hands under her top, sliding the fabric up over the twin peaks of her taut, firm breasts to reveal them to his famished gaze.

Even before he had touched her the heat of his bold, hungry stare made the sensitive peaks burn and harden into tight hard buds inside the light lacy covering.

The hunger in his eyes sent her spiralling out of control. She moaned low in her throat and sank her fingers into his hair as he unfastened her bra and cupped the warm mounds of aching flesh in his hands. Drawing them together, he buried his face in the softness before kneading the sensitised flesh and lashing the rosy tips with his tongue.

When he lifted his head there were dark bands of colour across his cheekbones and his eyes glowed as though lit from within.

'You are perfect!'

I *ought to be saying that,* Erin thought as he took her face between his hands and kissed her, because he was—totally and absolutely perfect.

After the kiss she didn't think much at all. She didn't even realise that he had removed her jeans until she felt the abrasive texture of his hair-roughened thighs against her bare skin.

As they continued to kiss with feverish abandon Erin's hands moved lower over his flat stomach, skimming then dipping below the waistband of his boxers, causing him to suck in his breath sharply.

'Is this what you want?' he asked thickly as he took her hand and fed it onto his body.

As he curved her fingers around the pulsing, engorged length of him Erin whimpered low in her throat and nodded. *'Yes.'* As she tightened her grip she felt the shudder ripple through his body.

'And do you want to feel me inside you?' He took her lower lip between his teeth, feeling the breath escape her mouth in a series of choky gasps. He nuzzled the side of her neck, breathing in the warm, aroused scent of her. 'Is that what you are imagining?'

'Oh, God!' she moaned, dragging his face up to hers. For a split second before her eyes closed he looked directly into the blazing blue of her eyes and saw some of the desperation he felt reflected in those shimmering depths. 'Yes, Francesco... yes,' she said before she sealed her open lips to his.

Parting her legs, he lowered himself between them and, running a hand down the curve of one thigh, he curved her leg over his hip, pulling her body up hard against him so that she could feel how much he wanted her.

'*Dio mio*, but I want you so badly...tell me you want me.'

Her eyes opened. The pupils were so dilated they almost swallowed up the blue. 'You know I do.'

'I want to hear you say it.'

Self-respect and pride were noble concepts, they might matter a lot in the cold light of day, but she was burning up from the inside out and nothing mattered at all except Francesco.

'I want you...' she whispered against his mouth.

As Francesco continued to kiss her his long, sensitive fingers moved in sensuous stroking motions along the curve of her inner thigh, advancing and retreating until, unable to bear the torment any longer, Erin took his hand and placed it against the damp curls at the apex of her legs.

'Please, Francesco,' she begged, kissing the sweat-slick column of his brown throat. '*I need...*'

'Oh, I *need* also, *bella mia,*' he responded thickly as he slid into her wetness. 'I need this.'

Erin, her head thrown back, a feral moan locked in her throat, arched and clutched at his shoulders as he thrust into her.

'That is... Oh, God...Francesco...you're...!' Her eyes closed tight as she concentrated on the feel of him filling her, her senses were sensually heightened to an almost unbearable degree as he moved.

'You feel...oh, God, Francesco...'

A moan vibrated in his chest as he felt her tighten hotly around him. He spoke in his own language, the words throaty and passionate spilling from him as he slid his hands under her bottom and lifted her up so that he could sink deeper into her.

Everything that wasn't Francesco, that wasn't his voice and his body, faded away. But as he took her to new heights of sensual pleasure one small stubborn portion of Erin's brain stayed removed from the devouring hunger that drove them both.

'Let go!' Francesco urged as if he sensed her holding back.

'I c…can't. I'll fall,' she heard herself pant stupidly against the sweat-slick column of his neck.

'Fall, *cara*. I will catch you.'

She shouldn't have believed him, but she did. A keening cry emerged from her parted lips as the pleasure exploded inside her, the sensation heightened when Francesco exploded, too.

CHAPTER TEN

ERIN had almost reached the bedroom door when she heard Francesco stir. His deep voice slurred with sleep, he asked, 'Where are you going?'

She turned back.

Francesco was raised on one elbow. The sheet that had been covering his body had slipped down to waist level. *Not* looking would have been too obvious, and also as it happened impossible.

He was quite simply magnificent.

She dragged her eyes back to his face, her colour significantly heightened, her expression carefully neutral.

'Back to my room.'

Even though they had just made love, looking at her staring at him with those big eyes sent a stab of desire through his body. He consulted the clock on the bedside table, and raised a brow in surprise when he saw four hours had elapsed since he had kicked the door closed.

He sprawled back with indolent grace and, allowing his eyes to travel up her body, thought about the taste of her, the silky softness of her skin as it glided against his own. 'What are you wearing?'

Erin touched a self-conscious, not quite steady hand to the lapel of the male shirt she wore. 'My things were wet.'

Sodden on the floor of the shower, to be precise, where they had fallen when he had stripped them from her body two hours earlier.

A memory surfaced in her head. A memory of Francesco standing in the shower, naked, his face lifted to the warm spray.

She had stood there mesmerised, unable to take her eyes off him until without warning his hand had shot out and he had dragged her inside under the warm jets of water.

'What are you doing?' she gasped, tilting her face up to his as she pushed the wet strands of water-darkened hair from her face. 'I told you it was a mistake. It can't happen again. I know it's totally my fault—'

'I think I had some minor input.'

'Valentina and Sam…the staff—they'll be back any time. I'm dressed,' she added weakly when none of the perfectly good reasons made any impact.

Francesco gave a wolfish smile that made her heartbeat quicken in anticipation. 'Not for long,' he promised.

'I'm out of here,' she retorted, blinking away the wetness from her lashes and not moving an inch.

She could see that lifting her arms as he peeled the wet top off might lead him to believe she wasn't totally serious in her threat. He might even imagine she wanted him to drop to his knees and pull her jeans and pants down over her hips. An impression that might have gained credence when she grabbed his head and moaned when he pressed his mouth into the damp curls he had exposed.

The memory of the hot, searing sensation as his tongue and fingers had slid between her thighs sent a wave of heat washing over her skin.

Closing her eyes, Erin pushed the erotic images from her head. The effort brought a visible sheen of moisture to her skin. 'I hope you don't mind…about the shirt.'

'Actually I do.'

Startled by his response, she narrowed her eyes warily.

'I think I might want to claim my property right now.'

Erin swallowed and crossed her hands over her chest in an unconsciously protective gesture.

'Are you talking about me or the shirt?' Her laugh only just stopped short of hysteria, but then trying to sound amused while she had a mental image of him slowly unpeeling the shirt to reveal her naked body had always been a non-starter.

One corner of his mouth lifted, but the smile didn't reach his eyes; they held a restive glitter that was in stark contrast to his indolent posture.

'I'll start with the shirt.' One hand tucked behind his head, he used the other to pat the bed that still bore the scent of her body. Erin wanted more than she could admit to respond to the invitation in his eyes. 'Come back to bed.'

Conflicting emotions were tearing her in several directions at once. Just looking at him awoke a lustful ache low in her abdomen. And imagining never spending another night in his arms filled her with panic.

At the same time she knew they had no future—the bottom line was he only wanted her back because of the baby.

'This shouldn't have happened.' Tears formed in her eyes because she didn't have the faintest idea where to go from here. 'Look, I'm not pretending it wasn't very—nice…'

A look of blank incredulity stole across his lean face. '*Nice*?' he echoed, pulling himself into a sitting position in one smooth motion that sent the quilt slithering to the floor exposing him totally.

She took refuge in flippancy. 'Well, what do you want me to say…that it was a life-changing experience?'

His face darkened with displeasure. 'Almost anything would be an improvement on "nice".' he snapped. 'Remind me not to come to you for a recommendation.'

Oblivious to his naked state, he swept aside the hank of silky dark hair that fell into his eyes.

'All right,' she conceded, her eyes falling to avoid the sardonic glitter in his stare. 'Relax, you were marvellous, though I had no idea that your ego required such delicate handling. Sex with you was always spectacular, but that's all it is.' It couldn't be anything else.

'You want more than I gave you?' he challenged with the arrogant confidence of a man who had heard the words of extravagant, breathless praise that had spilled unchecked from her lips when she had lain sated in his arms.

'I did. I don't anymore.' *Who are you trying to convince?*

Francesco studied her set face with a baffled expression. 'Could you be slightly less cryptic?'

'I loved you, I don't anymore, the sex is still great, but I can walk away.' *I just hope my knees heard that,* she thought, afraid that they were going to fold under her any minute. 'And I'm going to. I'm not going to Italy with you.'

He rose from the tumbled bed naked and breathtakingly magnificent to tower over her. 'You loved me, but you don't anymore, which is why you slept with me?' He shook his head slowly. 'Do you expect me to believe you mean a word of that? Or actually imagine I'm going to let you walk away with my child without a fight?'

She would have walked barefoot over hot coals before she let him see how much the warning scared her. 'I hope you're a good loser, Francesco.'

'I wouldn't know—I've not had any practice.'

And she believed him. 'You mean you're a bully.'

He watched one tear escape and slide down her cheek. 'If you think tears will work…'

'I'm not crying,' she denied huskily.

Another tear joined the first and, with a muffled curse, he turned away.

Erin wiped her cheek and watched uncertainly as he pulled a robe from the open wardrobe and belted it loosely around his waist.

When he turned back to her there was no trace of gloating male triumph remaining in his face, but there was something else, another emotion that eluded analysis.

He reached out and dabbed a tear from her cheek with the pad of his thumb. 'This is going to happen, Erin. Why don't you stop fighting it?'

Into the palpitating pause that followed his words there was a tap on the door followed by a female voice.

'Francesco?'

'My God!' Erin snapped, 'It's Valentina. She can't find me here like this!' she exclaimed, appalled at the idea.

'Why not?'

'Don't ask stupid questions,' Erin begged. 'I'd be mortified!'

'"Mortified?"' he echoed, a dark scowl forming on his lean features.

'Will you stop talking and just do something? Make her go away! Or…'

Francesco looked at her, smiled and cleared his throat. 'Come in, Valentina.'

Erin stared at him for a moment, transfixed in horror, before taking to her heels and fleeing to the bathroom. She stood there with her back against the wall, her heart hammering. It was several moments before she had regained enough composure to actively eavesdrop on the low-voiced conversation going on in the other room and then it turned out to be mostly in Italian.

Just as she was about to give up on trying to figure out what they were saying she heard Francesco say in English 'No, Erin doesn't blame you at all.'

'Well, I hope not. I really hope you two sort things out, Francesco. In my opinion Erin is the best thing that has ever happened to you. Just don't rush things; give her time. You can't just click your fingers and expect her to come running,' she scolded.

Erin gave a mortified grimace at an image of the tumbled bedclothes in her mind. Click his fingers   he hadn't even had to make that much effort!

'Rafael·would have liked her, don't you think?'

Erin, picking up on the name she had never heard before, waited curiously to hear Francesco's reply. It was a long time coming.

'Rafe would have loved her.'

A few remarks in Italian followed. Erin listened with half an ear wondering about the odd note in Francesco's voice.

She waited until she heard the door close behind Valentina before walking back into the room. Francesco was sitting on the bed.

'Who is Rafe?' she asked.

He gave a thin-lipped smile. 'You heard that, then?'

'It was hard not to.'

'Rafe was my twin brother.'

She was totally stunned by the information. 'You have a brother…a *twin*? Why didn't you ever mention—?'

In a voice that was flat and totally expressionless he cut across her. 'Had. Rafe died.'

Erin gulped and swallowed, her blue eyes softening with compassion as she went to sit beside him on the bed. 'Oh, Francesco, I'm sorry. I had no idea.'

Though he didn't respond directly, he picked his wallet up from the bedside table and, withdrawing a snapshot, handed it to her without comment.

The edges of the snapshot were creased and curled as though it had been fingered a lot, but the faces of the two young men in the photo were clear. Francesco was standing, his brother sitting. Francesco had his arm slung across the shoulders of his brother. They were both laughing.

'You were identical twins!'

My God, it would be bad enough to lose a sibling, but she couldn't even begin to imagine the horror of losing an identical twin.

'Almost nobody could tell us apart.'

Erin was surprised to hear him say this. To her mind the differences between the two men were obvious. Francesco's mouth was wider and firmer and his chin more squarely resolute. His brother's features were probably more regular, and to her seemed softer and less aggressively masculine.

'I'm sorry, I had no idea…'

When Francesco turned his head and looked at her the emptiness in his eyes frightened her. Her heart aching with empathy, she reached across and laid her hand over his.

'We looked alike, but that was on the surface. We weren't really alike at all.' He took the photo from her fingers and looked at it. 'Rafe was the imaginative, sensitive one. I'll show you some of his paintings some time if you like. He was very talented.'

'He was an artist?'

'He did a lot of things; he was…restless. I think our parents thought that marriage would make him settle down.'

'He was married?'

Francesco, his expression darkening, nodded. 'He was, but it was not a success. Rafe spent four years trying to cling to her, desperately trying to change himself into the sort of man she wanted him to be.'

It had destroyed him.

It was obvious from the tension in Francesco's manner that he didn't enjoy speaking about his brother. Erin hesitated before gently asking, 'How did he die?'

'He killed himself.'

A short static silence followed his abrupt and shocking words. A tiny gasp escaped Erin's parted lips.

'He took an overdose.'

She lifted a hand to her mouth and her blue eyes filled with tears of sympathy.

'When I found him he looked as if he was sleeping. He looked so peaceful,' Francesco recalled.

Erin's eyes widened with horror. Not only had his twin killed himself, Francesco had found the body! She ached to comfort him, but what, she wondered, could you say that didn't sound like a pathetic platitude?

'He came to see me, you know, earlier that week asking for my advice.'

That in itself had not been unusual. His twin had *always* turned up when he'd had a problem; admittedly sometimes Francesco had had trouble recognising the things Rafe had lost sleep over as problems. And if he was brutally honest with himself the dramatic spin his brother had put on relatively trivial incidents had frequently annoyed him.

It seemed to him that Rafe had lurched from one drama to another. Rafe didn't meet a beautiful woman, he met a *goddess!*

Francesco had never met a goddess and he had definitely never felt the desire to place a woman on a pedestal. When Rafe had only half-jokingly accused him of having no soul he had not disagreed.

'You want to know what I told him? What I told my suicidal brother?' Erin shook her head and felt totally inadequate in the face of the anguish that was written in every line of his face. 'I said, "Pull yourself together, Rafe." I told him that people don't die of broken hearts, but it turned out they do.'

The official verdict, of course, had been different.

It had emerged at the inquest that Rafe had recently been diagnosed with bipolar disorder and had convinced his doctors he had been taking his medication for the condition. His family, Francesco included, had known nothing about his disorder and this, they had concluded, had been the main factor that had led to his tragic suicide.

But Francesco knew different; he could have changed things. He *should* have changed things.

Horror-stricken, Erin could only sit and listen as the words spilled from him. She had the impression he had forgotten she was even there; it made her wonder how long he'd had these feelings locked inside.

'My brother needed me and all I could come up with was worthless platitudes.' His voice shook with self-loathing. 'He loved that woman more than life itself and I said, "Don't sit there moping. Be tough—go and get her." So he did and she told him that she loved someone else and he killed himself.'

As he closed his eyes Francesco's head fell forward. She watched his shoulders heave. 'You stupid idiot, Rafe! *Dio,* what a waste. What a total bloody waste!' he raged.

Unable to bear his pain any longer, Erin got to her knees on the bed and came up behind him, pressing her body up against the curve of his spine and, resting her head against his neck, linked her hands across his chest.

It was little enough but the physical contact seemed to help him regain some degree of control over his emotions because the shudders that racked his body gradually stopped.

As he straightened up Erin loosed her grip and leaned back on her heels, her grave blue eyes trained on his face as he swept the blue-black hair back from his brow.

'I can't even begin to imagine what it must feel like…' she said softly.

'You really want to know?' he yelled, turning his seething anger on her. 'Will that satisfy your grubby, prurient curiosity? You're just like all the others, pretending sympathy while enjoying the misfortunes of another!'

Erin flinched at the bile in his tone but did not try and defend herself or protest this very black view of human nature.

'If you want to tell me, Francesco.'

She realised he had never stopped blaming himself for his brother's death.

'I wake up every morning and there's a dark empty space inside me…a black hole.' He pressed a hand to his chest and turned eyes that were filled with bitter self-reproach to Erin. 'It hurts knowing that I will never see him again, never hear his voice again, and the worst part is I could have stopped it. I *should* have known.' He swallowed, the muscles in his brown throat working as he closed his eyes.

Hand pressed to her mouth, Erin watched as he fought to regain control. She was shocked and horrified. How long, she wondered, had he been carrying around this guilt and pain?

'It never even occurred to me that he was ill.'

Certainly when Rafe had turned up at his place looking the personification of a tragic hero Francesco had been more irritated than alarmed. The state of his brother's marriage, like his mood, had see-sawed violently between bliss and dark, brooding despair.

'Why didn't I see that his mood swings were getting worse?'

'Why should you?'

Francesco's head came up; he gave her a guarded look. '*Why*?'

'Yes, why?'

'I should have.'

'We don't analyse minutely the behaviour of the people close to us.'

'Maybe Rafe didn't want me to see, and who could blame him? It's not as if I'd been wildly sympathetic before.'

Erin flung up her hands in frustrated exasperation. Francesco seemed totally determined to blame himself for what had happened to his twin. 'Did you tell him everything?'

Francesco dismissed the question with an impatient gesture. 'That's not the same thing. If he hadn't felt he had to hide his illness from me…' teeth clenched, his features rigid, he ground his clenched fist into the bed frame '…if I had known I would have made sure he took his medication. If I'd thought before I doled out advice Rafe might still be alive.'

'That's a lot of ifs, Francesco. When bad things happen we look for a reason,' she began, choosing her words with care. 'It's human nature, but sometimes,' she said sadly, 'there simply isn't one to find. Bad things just happen; they happen to good people who don't deserve it. You can't blame yourself for what happened to your twin, Francesco. It isn't your fault.'

He gave a twisted smile. 'That's what the doctors said,' he admitted. 'They talked about chemical imbalances, but it wasn't a chemical imbalance in his blood that killed Rafe; it was black despair.' His voice shook with the depth of his feelings and raw emotion. 'And I stood by and watched it happen.'

Erin could not bear to hear any more of this. 'That's nonsense and you know it!' she protested. 'Do you really think your brother would want you to beat yourself up over this?' she demanded.

He looked startled by the question. 'I never really…'

'Thought about it like that? Well, that's obvious, because if you had you'd have realised that he wouldn't have any more than you would have wanted him to if the situation had been reversed.'

'Rafe was always there for me. He always had time for me…'

'This hair-shirt look really doesn't suit you, Francesco. In fact all this self-flagellation is pretty self-indulgent.' Ashamed of yelling at him when she ought to have been soothing him, she added a guilty-sounding, 'Sorry.'

He schooled his laboured breathing to something that approached normality. 'No, it is I who should be sorry.' It might be his imagination but Francesco was conscious of feeling— for want of a better word—*lighter* than he had in a long time.

'What for? I'm the one who scolded you.'

'I needed scolding,' he reflected, a shadow of a smile lifting the sombreness of his expression. 'You're right—I am wallowing in self-pity.'

'I didn't say that.'

'No?' He arched a dark brow and shrugged, one corner of his sensual mouth lifting in a crooked smile that just tore at her sensitive heart. 'Maybe you should have. Erin, the things I said…' he began, his manner uncharacteristically awkward as he met her eyes. 'I should not have shouted at you… The thing is it is difficult for me to speak of my feelings. Rafe used to say that my aura—he was very into that sort of stuff—must have so many "keep out" signs that it would take a very brave person to get close to me.'

His dark eyes flickered across her face before his chin dropped to his chest. 'Someone who goes where angels fear to tread,' had been Rafe's exact words.

'Or a really stupid one,' she muttered under her breath as she drew back the fingers that hovered just above his dark hair. Her heart ached to see him so vulnerable. 'It must have been a terrible time for you and your family,' she said huskily.

'It was not good.' He gave a twisted smile. 'But at the time there were things to do…arrangements…no time to think. Later it was harder and my parents took it very badly.'

And everyone expected Francesco to cope, Erin thought, looking at his broad shoulders and thinking of the problems people offloaded on them.

'My mother especially…' He lifted his head, dragging a hand through his tousled dark hair before revealing, 'There was always a special bond between her and Rafe.' Nothing in his expression or manner suggested he had in any way resented this special relationship. 'She hasn't been the same since.'

'She still has you!' The indignant protest died on Erin's tongue when, without warning, he reached across and took her face between his hands.

'You had me, too, *cara*, but you didn't want me.'

Didn't want him? God, if only that were true. If she had ever fooled herself into believing she didn't love him the last few minutes had destroyed that illusion. Seeing the depth of pain in his eyes had torn at her heart. She had felt his grief and loss as though it had been her own…and had felt helpless.

If she could have she would have taken his pain on herself.

And yet she was about to add to it by taking away his chance to be a full-time father.

She just couldn't do that to him; Francesco had lost enough without losing his child.

'I always wanted you, Francesco.' *And I'll always love you!*

Francesco's eyes darkened and a muscle in his lean cheek clenched as he sucked in a deep breath. '*Erin…*' His hands slid to her shoulders as he said something thick in his own language. As he bent his head towards hers Erin closed her eyes, her eyelashes fluttering like butterfly wings against her flushed cheeks.

'Perhaps we could make a go of it?'

Francesco's hands fell away and his head came up with a jerk. His dark eyes raked her face with an intensity she found hard to endure. 'You are agreeing to come back to Italy with me?'

My God, is that what I'm doing? Do I really want to be pregnant in a foreign country loving a man who only wants me back because of the child I'm carrying?

'I'm prepared to give it a go, for the sake of the baby.' *You are crazy, Erin.* 'But the secrets have to stop. And don't say there were no secrets, because our marriage was based on a tissue of lies and omissions from day one. You never once mentioned your twin…'

'I suppose it was a relief to be with someone who didn't know about Rafe, to escape the interminable sympathy. The conversations that stopped when I walked into a room. Death is one of the last taboo subjects in our society. It makes people uncomfortable to be around someone who is bereaved. They either gush or cross the street to avoid you.'

'When did he…when did Rafe die?' She could actually see how a man like Francesco, a man who was fiercely private and self-contained, might find well-wishers intrusive.

'Six months ago.'

'Six months!' No wonder Francesco's feelings were so raw. 'That's no time at all...' she began, then stopped, the colour seeping from her face.

That meant that when she had met Francesco his brother had only been dead for three months.

Their meeting. The whirlwind romance, the reckless dash into marriage—all suddenly made a horrible kind of sense.

The behaviour she had attributed to a man in love could equally be attributed to a man unwilling to confront his feelings.

Some men in similar circumstances might have turned to drink or relied on prescription drugs.

In Francesco's case he had turned to her!

It all made perfect horrible sense!

Francesco, half out of his head with grief and unwilling to acknowledge his feelings of anger and guilt, had used anything to distract himself. She had been the ultimate distraction and he had used her to ease the pain he was going through. Not consciously—she did not believe he was capable of being that callous.

Had he already begun to realise that he didn't really love her the night of the ball? It would explain why he had not done more to stop her going. Sure, his pride had been hurt that it had been her who had walked away, but maybe deep down he had been secretly relieved? Until he had found out about the baby.

'You're cold,' Francesco said as she shivered.

She gave a forced smile and stood up, clutching the robe tight around her. 'A little.'

'Are you all right?'

'Fine. I think I'll go change.'

'You can keep the shirt.'

My heart for your shirt. The exchange hardly seemed fair. Repressing the hysterical laugh that was lodged in her throat, she nodded tightly and left the room.

CHAPTER ELEVEN

ERIN managed to maintain a shaky illusion of composure until she was safely in her own room. Once there she sank onto the bed with her head in her hands.

Her face was tear-stained when a few minutes later she lifted her head and exclaimed out loud, 'Oh, my God, I really said I'd go back to Italy with him.'

Walking over to the old-fashioned washstand, she turned on the cold tap and splashed her face with water. There were water droplets trembling on her lashes as she looked at herself in the mirror. The indent between her feathery brows deepened as she sighed.

How did I manage to fool myself? she wondered. It seemed incredible that she had for one moment believed that just because it would be convenient she had fallen out of love with Francesco.

Love didn't work that way; at least it didn't for her. The important thing now was that she didn't lose sight of the fact that love didn't automatically equate with happy ever after, especially when the object of your affections had never really been in love with you in the first place.

No more self-delusion—she had to see things as they really were, she told herself sternly.

The problem was that seeing things as they were did not

produce any magical solution. As she dried her face and applied a thin layer of concealing tinted moisturiser Erin nursed the depressing knowledge that there was no solution, magical or mundane.

God, this was a nightmare!

Her troubled gaze trained on the horses in the paddock underneath her window, she lifted her chin. Perhaps it was best not to try and think of a solution to everything, just concentrate instead on sorting one problem at a time.

The scene on the patio when she went downstairs was of domestic harmony. Sam was seated on a wrought-iron chair reading the newspaper while his wife was irritating him by reading aloud headlines that caught her eyes.

It was the sight of Francesco sitting on a rug spread on the grass, making baby Gianni, who was kicking his legs, chuckle by blowing raspberries on his bare tummy that stopped Erin in her tracks.

The hand around her heart tightened as she watched him. He would make the most incredible father.

Valentina was the first to notice her. 'Erin! Grab a scone before this greedy piglet scoffs the lot,' she said, ruffling her husband's hair.

Erin glanced towards the plate of scones liberally laced with cream and shook her head. 'No, thanks.' She made a conscious effort to look anywhere but at Francesco, who had turned his head when Valentina had called her name.

Erin looked at the spot on the rug that Francesco patted. She slipped off her shoes and began to walk towards him across the wet grass. Just looking at him made her ache with love. It was a mystery how she had ever managed to fool herself she could ever feel anything else for him…

Before she reached them her phone began to ring. She gave an apologetic grimace and pulled it from her pocket. 'It's Mum,' she said, pretending not to notice the looks her hosts exchanged at the information. 'I'll just take it…' She gave a vague gesture towards the house and walked barefoot in that direction.

Once out of sight of the group she lifted the phone to her ear. 'Damn, no signal!' She gave a frustrated sigh and looked around. She spotted the flight of stone steps that led to the room above where Sam stored the horses' feed and headed for it at a fast trot.

She slipped on her shoes before running lightly up the steps. At the top she scanned the screen on her phone and gave a sigh of relief when she saw she had a signal.

'Mum, what's wrong?' It was safe to assume that something was wrong—her mother had a talent for timing her crises to coincide with social occasions. A less generous person might have suspected she timed it deliberately!

Erin sat on the top step and listened with more resignation than concern—she'd been there too many times before to panic—as her tearful mother explained between sobs that her father had walked out.

'I'll be right th—' She let out a startled yelp as the phone was pulled unceremoniously from her fingers. She lifted her head in time to see Francesco lift it to his ear.

'No, Erin won't be there. She has a previous engagement.'

'What do you think you're doing?' she yelled furiously.

'Something you should have done a long time ago—cut the apron strings,' he informed her callously.

Erin rose to her feet quivering with indignation. Though he was standing a couple of steps below her she still had to tilt her head to look him in the face. 'How *dare* you? You had no right! She was in a *terrible* state; she needs me.'

'No, she uses you,' he contradicted.

'You're talking about my mother.'

'And she'll carry on using you,' he said, ignoring her furious insertion, 'until you break the cycle. It's about habit and guilt. If you go every time your mother calls you're simply reinforcing her behaviour.'

Her eyes flashing dangerously in response to his extraordinarily high-handed attitude, she glared up at him. 'And if I let you run my life and decide who I talk to I'm simply reinforcing your inclination to be a total despot!' she yelled back. 'My mother *needs* me.'

'So does your family.'

'But she is my…' Lower lip caught between her teeth, she shook her head as she caught his meaning.

'The baby and I…we are your family now, Erin. What are you going to do when the baby is born? Drop everything including him when she calls?' he suggested bitterly.

She felt as though she were being torn in two directions. At one level she knew he was right—he was after all only echoing thoughts she had had herself. But she resented him for making his point this way, for making no allowances for her feelings.

'The situation is untenable, Erin,' he said quietly.

Did he think she didn't know that? 'I feel responsible.'

'Get over it,' he recommended unsympathetically. He tossed the phone and she automatically caught it. 'If you don't like the situation you can change it—the choice is yours.'

Some choice, she thought, staring at the phone in her hand.

'You're asking me to choose between my mother and you.'

He shrugged. 'It is not something you should have to think about.'

'You have no right to ask me!' she quivered, lifting a hand to her head. 'You're just as bad,' she accused shrilly, 'as she is! Get out of my way. I've had enough of this!'

'That's right,' he jeered. 'If things get difficult or even mildly uncomfortable, run away.'

'"Mildly uncomfortable!"' she yelled back. 'Maybe this is a minor irritation to you—'

'You've never been a *minor* anything!' he retorted.

Her mistake, Erin decided when analysing the moment at a later date, was turning her head to look back at him as she ducked under his arm to reach the next step. If she hadn't she would have been able to regain her balance when her heels snagged in the hem of her jeans and she wouldn't have taken a dive down the shallow flight of stone stairs and ended in an inelegant heap on the floor on the cobbled yard below.

She lay there, winded, her eyes wide open. As she struggled to get her breath she was aware of Francesco falling to his knees beside her.

'Are you all right?' Without waiting for her to respond, he added furiously, '*Dio*! You little idiot! What the hell did you think you were doing!' Before she had either the breath or the opportunity to respond Francesco launched into a low, incensed sounding tirade in Italian.

Erin only understood one word in three, but one sentiment she did pick out was a very heartfelt wish that he had never set eyes on her.

'And I,' she gasped, hoping he attributed the weak tears that flooded her eyes to pain. 'wish I'd never laid eyes on you, either.'

'You just threw yourself headlong down a flight of stairs. You could have killed yourself, and what about the baby?'

'There was no *throwing* involved. I just fell over my own

feet.' Clumsy, she was willing to admit to, but not stupid! 'And it wouldn't have happened in the first place if you hadn't been…' She stopped, wide eyes lifting to his face. 'Oh, my God, the baby!' She tried to ease her weight off one hip and winced. The cramping pain that extended like a band around her middle made her gasp.

'You *are* hurt!'

She was, but it wasn't her own safety that Erin was worrying about.

'Here, let me help you.'

She shook her head. 'I think I might stay here for a moment.' Please, *please*, God, make the baby all right.

If anything happened to it she would never forgive herself.

'What is it? What's wrong?'

'I think perhaps you should call an ambulance, just as a precaution.'

Even before she had finished speaking he had his phone out and was punching in the emergency number.

'Ambulance,' he snapped. 'The nature of the emergency? My wife has fallen down a flight of stairs. No, she's conscious and…look, she's twelve weeks pregnant. Just get here.' He gave the address before sliding his phone back into his pocket. 'They said just stay still.'

Erin nodded as he pushed the hair back from her brow with cool brown fingers. 'Pretty much what I planned to do. You know I'm sure everything's fine.'

'Of course it is,' he agreed.

If it wasn't—his firm jaw tightened as he pushed aside the thought he wouldn't permit himself to contemplate such a possibility.

'I'm just being c-cautious.' Erin strove to hide her terror, but it was a struggle.

'You want this baby a lot, don't you?'

'Yes, I do.' She wanted this baby with a ferocity that she had not imagined she was capable of. She might not be able to have the man, but the baby was hers.

He reached out tentatively towards her stomach and then drew back. 'Are you still in pain?'

'A little,' she admitted. 'I think I must have caught my side on the bottom step.'

Francesco looked at the sharp edge and cursed under his breath. When he turned back to Erin she was dabbing the tip of her tongue to the beads of sweat along her upper lip. He had no doubt at all she was playing down her symptoms for his benefit.

'You will make them save my baby, won't you, Francesco, if I'm out of it for any reason?'

Francesco, pale under his tan, closed his eyes. 'You won't be out of it,' he told her hoarsely.

'But just in case,' she persisted.

'I will do everything that is necessary.' *To keep you safe and well*, he added silently.

The ambulance arrived a few minutes later. Francesco watched, feeling increasingly useless as they loaded Erin into the back of the ambulance. Before getting in himself, Francesco babbled a brief explanation to a shocked and concerned Sam and Valentina who had appeared.

The presence at Erin's side of a paramedic who monitored her condition meant he couldn't even hold her hand. Once they reached the hospital casualty department the situation got, if anything, more frustrating. She was whisked away immediately, while they expected him to be content with a promise from a harassed-looking doctor that they would tell him as soon as they knew anything.

Francesco was not content.

He was expressing his discontent to an officious and most obstructive person whose name badge identified him as some sort of administrator when a doctor older than the one who had spoken to him earlier approached.

'Mr Romanelli, is it?'

Francesco took the hand extended to him.

'James Ross.'

'What is happening to my wife?' The conspiracy of silence was driving him crazy. Did these people not appreciate that with no information it was natural to assume the worst? 'I need to be with her.'

The doctor gave a soothing smile. 'And you shall be,' he promised. 'Come with me—we'll go somewhere a little more private.'

Wasn't that what they said in medical dramas before they broke bad news?

Francesco refused tea, refused a seat, and explained that the only thing he was interested in was information concerning his wife's well-being.

'Yes, well, I'm afraid that your wife has some internal bleeding.'

He looked understanding as Francesco, deathly pale beneath his naturally vibrant colouring, sank into the chair he had just rejected.

Francesco had felt like this only once before. On that occasion he could remember thinking that a man could only endure this sort of pain once. Yet here he was alive and feeling as if someone had pushed their hand into his chest and ripped out his heart.

'That is bad?'

'Well, any surgical intervention carries a risk.'

The breath left Francesco's body in a long shuddering sigh. 'You mean you can do something?'

'Good Lord, yes! I'm sorry I wasn't clear.'

Francesco suspected it was his mental acuity and not the doctor's communication skills that were at fault.

'Hopefully we will be able to perform the procedure via a laparoscope—no need, you understand, for an incision? That is the method of choice, but there are no guarantees. Depending on what we find, we might have to go in.

'Your wife is very concerned about what the operation will mean for the baby, but I have made it quite plain to her that there is really no option.'

'The baby is all right—alive?' Amazement swept over him. 'I assumed when you said…'

'No, your baby is doing very well, and there is no reason that it should not survive the surgery without taking any harm. Though again, and I emphasise this, there are no guarantees.'

'But it has a fighting chance?' If anything happened to the baby, Erin would never forgive him—he would never forgive himself!

'Absolutely. Now would you like to see your wife?'

Francesco leapt to his feet. 'I would.'

The doctor spoke into an intercom and a nurse appeared. 'Would you take Mr Romanelli to his private room to see his wife?'

CHAPTER TWELVE

THE room was little more than a box, white and clinical. Francesco approached silently. Erin appeared to be sleeping, or possibly they had given her something to make her sleep? As he looked at her lying there she seemed so small and scarily fragile with an intravenous infusion attached to her arm.

Francesco stood at the bedside, his chest tight with the emotions that swelled and grew as he looked at her.

The cover was white, the gown she wore was white and her skin was if possible even whiter, her freckles standing out in stark relief across the bridge of her nose! The only colour was her glorious hair that peeked out beneath the ridiculous cap they had put on her head.

He closed his eyes. His silent prayer was interrupted by the sound of a slurred voice.

'You look terrible.'

He opened his eyes and saw her looking up at him.

'I thought you were asleep.'

She shook her head and made a weak flailing gesture, which he correctly interpreted as an effort to catch hold of his hand. Francesco caught her hand between the two of his.

'They gave me something. I feel a bit drunk...do I sound a bit drunk?'

Francesco smiled into her glazed eyes. 'A little,' he admitted.

'Thought so… Did they tell you?'

He nodded. 'You'll be fine,' he promised.

'And the baby will be fine?' She looked at him with total trust that pierced him like a knife. He didn't deserve her trust—if it hadn't been for him there would have been no accident.

'Absolutely,' he said, hoping with all his heart that he was right.

Erin gave a sigh. 'Good. Do you know that you have the most incredible…no, better than incredible mouth?' she slurred.

'Thank you.'

'I like your eyes, too.'

Before she had commented on any other parts of his anatomy two porters and a nurse arrived with a trolley.

They let him walk with them as far as the entrance to the anaesthetic room. She lay with her eyes closed, her small hand tightly curled over his.

He bent and kissed her lips before they wheeled her inside, resisting the urge he had to yell at the person who removed her hand from his.

As they closed the door the last thing he heard was a slurred, 'And great legs, too!'

The first thing Erin became conscious of was voices, male and female; she couldn't understand what they were saying.

'Go away,' she said crankily. 'My head hurts. I'm thirsty.' She lifted a hand to protect her eyes from the strong light shining in them. 'Where am I?'

Someone spoke, Erin heard them say, 'She's back with us,' and there was a click and light filtering through her fingers vanished.

The next thing that Erin was conscious of was fingers,

cool on her forehead. They stilled for a moment. She tried to say don't stop but her vocal chords did not respond. She struggled to open her eyes but gave up—her eyelids felt too heavy, and besides the soothing, cool fingers were stroking again.

'If anything happened to you...*per amor di Dio,* I would never have forgiven myself.' Francesco, his lean face contorted with self-recrimination, looked down at the pale, still-sleeping features of the woman he had married.

The woman he had nearly lost.

His tortured eyes darkened and he tensed expectantly as her eyelashes fluttered against the pallor of her waxen cheek. A sigh escaped him when after a moment they stilled and there was no other sign of returning consciousness.

A nurse materialised quietly at the bottom of the bed.

'Shouldn't she be awake by now?' he asked, anxiety making his manner abrupt.

The nurse gave a soothing smile and promised him everything was just as it ought to be. 'She'll probably sleep until the morning,' she informed him with a lot more cheer than he considered the situation warranted. 'If she does wake up she'll be pretty woozy. Maybe you should go home and get some sleep?'

He reacted irritably to the tentative suggestion. 'I'll stay.'

After studying his face she did not argue the point. 'Would you like a blanket?'

'I do not need a blanket.' What he needed was his wife to open her eyes.

'I'll get you another coffee,' the nurse offered, before scribbling something on the chart and leaving the room.

Francesco got up and began to pace the room, his expression distracted. Despite the constant reassurances from the medical staff that the operation had been a total success he would not, *could* not relax until Erin woke up. Until he heard her voice.

'Though when you do wake up,' he said, dropping heavily back into the chair that was drawn up to the bed, 'you will probably tell me you hate me.' He rested his chin on his steepled fingers and shook his head. 'And I wouldn't blame you. First Rafe and now you. A man should cherish those who are most precious to him. But no, I had to prove a point, make you choose me. *Dio,* but I am a total selfish bastard! I promise you that when you are well I will…if anything ever happened to you…' He picked up the small hand that lay against the sheet and lifted it to his lips. 'I swear I will never let anything hurt you again.'

'Mr Romanelli…'

He started at the sound of the nurse's voice and, first laying Erin's hand gently back down onto the bed, turned his head.

'I'll leave the coffee here, shall I?' she said, placing the cup on the bedside table.

'Thank you,' he said, turning back to Erin and covering her small hand with his. The wave of emotion he felt as he looked at her was like a physical pain.

'I can't lose you.'

'I'm not lost.'

'Erin?' Relief flooded through him as she opened her eyes and looked up at him.

'Hello, *cara,*' he said thickly.

'Francesco?'

Her blurry vision cleared and Erin found herself looking into his unmistakable features. His face, his fallen dark angel face, looked drawn and almost haggard, he hadn't shaved and there were deep lines bracketing his mouth that she couldn't recall seeing before.

'We got married, didn't we? That was so stupid.' She closed

her eyes and did not see the spasm of pain that contorted his lean features. 'You make a much better lover than I make a wife. Did something happen?'

Francesco swallowed, seeing in his head her fall down those steps. 'Yes, *cara*, you fell.'

'I've got a sore throat, too. Fall? I don't remember,' she complained crankily.

'That doesn't matter now; you sleep.' He reached for the buzzer to summon a nurse. Where was the damned woman?

She sighed as she felt his cool fingers on her forehead. She smiled sleepily. 'That's nice. I had a dream someone was stroking my head. It was nice; was it you?'

'Go to sleep.'

'Will you be here when I wake up?'

'I'm not going anywhere.'

She smiled, expelled a deep sigh and almost immediately fell asleep.

'When can I go home?'

'I'm beginning to get the impression you don't like us,' teased the doctor who had just declared the puncture wounds on her abdomen, the only external sign of the emergency surgery she had undergone, were fine.

'You've only been with us forty-eight hours.'

'It feels like longer.'

The doctor laughed. 'We just need to monitor the baby overnight. I don't foresee any problem there…tough little beggar, that one,' he said, peering at the heartbeat tracery in his hand. 'As for you, young lady…'

'I feel fine,' she said.

'No need to look so worried—that was my diagnosis, too.'

After scribbling something on her chart the doctor left, two nurses in tow, and she settled down to read one of the magazines from the stack on the bedside locker.

She was unable to concentrate, and her eyes drifted around the private room, which still resembled a florists' shop even after she had sent a pile of flowers to the oncology ward. A frown of discontent furrowed her brow and pulled down the corners of her mouth as she heard the sound of voices in the corridor outside.

Being in this room resembled being stranded on a desert island, albeit a desert island with room service. The fact you could hear the rest of the world getting on with its collective life made the sense of isolation all the more intense.

It wasn't that she wasn't *grateful,* but she was dying of boredom.

When she had said as much that morning Francesco had responded with a very unsympathetic and pretty brutal, 'Well, that is preferable to being dead!'

He made it sound as if she didn't know how lucky she was, which she did. But a person couldn't go on getting misty about being alive. They had to get on with living! Though she sensed she might have a fight on her hands on that score, Francesco was showing some dangerous signs of wrapping her in cotton wool.

That first night it had been around four in the morning when she had come to properly. She had some dim recollection of wakening earlier but the memory was confused and tangled up in her dreams.

She could remember the relief that had swept over her when she had opened her eyes and seen him.

Her first thought had been for the baby and even before she had asked the question uppermost in her thoughts Francesco had told her what she had needed to know.

'The baby is fine and so,' he added, smoothing the hair from her brow, 'are you. Shall I call the nurse? Do you have pain?'

She lifted a hand that had a drip attached to it to her forehead. 'I'm not sure. I feel a bit…spaced.'

'That is probably the injection they gave you a while back.'

'Have you been here all the time?' How long that was she had no idea. 'Injection?' She struggled to think past the cotton wool her brain appeared to be stuffed with. 'Should they be giving me drugs with the baby…are you sure he's all right?' she croaked, trying to raise herself up.

'I am positive the baby is fine. Listen, there,' he said, pressing a finger to his lips to urge her to silence. 'You hear it?'

'That's the baby's heartbeat?'

He nodded.

She gulped as hot, emotional tears filled her eyes. 'That is so incredible.'

'It is, and they would not give you medication that would harm the baby.

Erin sighed and let the tension leave her body. 'I'd never have forgiven myself if…' She stopped and closed her eyes with a groan.

'It wasn't *your* fault.'

She turned her head on the pillow and looked at him.

His appearance had shocked her. With his normally sleek hair standing up in spiky tufts and his skin tinged an unhealthy grey, he looked a million miles from his sleek, perfectly groomed normal self.

She closed her eyes, temporarily drained of the energy required to keep them open. She had no idea how long she dozed, drifting in and out of sleep, but it was some time and several blood-pressure checks later that she came to fully.

Francesco was *still* there. He was even in her dreams.

'You do know you look shocking?'

'You don't look too hot yourself.'

'I have an excuse—I've just had surgery,' she teased.

'And I've just spent hours wondering if my wife and child will live.' The words he had obviously struggled to contain emerged from between clenched teeth.

'Don't you think it might be an idea for you to go home, get some sleep?'

'Perhaps,' he conceded. 'Is there anything I can get you before I go?'

'My mouth is so dry—do you suppose that I could have something to drink?'

'I don't know, but I'll ask.'

'When can I go home?'

'It is as I suspected...'

'What is?'

'You're going to be an awkward patient, the demanding sort that nurses avoid.'

He did go, but returned looking much more like himself a few hours later.

Of course, she had not made the mistake of imagining that she was the draw that brought him back again and again.

It was the baby.

Several of the nurses had remarked on his devotion, and his smouldering Latin looks had come into the conversation on more than one occasion! Though most were too tactful to lust after him in front of her, Erin was pretty sure her husband had caused more than a few hearts to flutter in the hospital corridors.

One young student who was particularly smitten somehow always found a reason to be in her room when Francesco happened to be there. That morning when she had been taking

Erin's temperature she had wondered why Erin did not have a picture of her husband by her bed.

'But I suppose you're not likely to forget what he looks like, are you? He's always here.' The wistful envy in her voice made Erin smile.

'I bet he'll make a great dad. Italian men are good with children, aren't they?'

An image of Francesco sprawled on a rug playing with little Gianni popped into her head. 'Some are,' she agreed, wondering how this young girl would react if she told her that her marriage, far from being what it looked from the outside, was nothing but a sham!

The only reason Francesco had come back was because he had found out about the baby. And there was no question in her mind that if it hadn't been for her pregnancy he wouldn't be refusing to consider a divorce.

He had been experiencing the emotional backlash of his twin's death when they had met, which totally explained the entire mad, reckless rush into marriage with someone he barely knew. If she hadn't left when she had he would most likely have woken up one morning and thought, *What the hell have I done?* And then things would have taken their natural course.

She had tried the previous evening to tell him that he could have his freedom. He had stared at her in a particularly daunting manner while she had outlined her, admittedly pretty sketchy, plan of moving to Italy so that he could have easier access to his child.

He didn't seem grateful for the concession she was willing to make. Neither had he held back when he had expressed his blighting opinion of her plan!

'No, I do *not* think it is a good idea. I think it is a ridiculous idea. I'm sorry, Erin, if you find the thought of living as my wife so distasteful, but I suggest you put these wild and im-practical notions from your mind. You will be living with me as my wife; we will be a family.' He effectively silenced further protests by adding, 'This is something you will do because I know that you have the best interests of our child at heart.'

If all else failed, use emotional blackmail—and why not? she thought bleakly. It had worked.

It was obvious to Erin that once she went back to Italy with him Francesco would resist using every resource, which in his case were pretty much limitless, any attempt she made to remove their child from the country. And the thing was she loved him and wanted to be with him so much that part of her just wanted to go with the flow and stop resisting even though she knew that he didn't love her.

And that being the case there was every chance that one day he would fall in love with someone else.

She spent most of the afternoon wondering if she was being totally insane for returning to Italy with him. Finally with a spinning head she picked up a book, in the vain hope of dis-tracting herself from thoughts of her personal life.

It was around four and she was staring blankly at the same page she had been for the past ten minutes when there was a tentative knock on the door.

The man who walked in was a little above medium height. He had a beard, slightly receding hair and wore glasses.

She had never seen him before.

'Mrs Romanelli...' He approached the bed beaming with his hand outstretched.

A bemused Erin gave him her hand. 'I'm sorry. I don't—?'

'Stupid of me, I should have introduced myself. Peter Heyer.'

Clearly he expected it to mean something to her. Erin shook her head. 'I'm sorry, I—'

'Sorry, I assumed that Francesco would have explained things to you.'

'Are you a lawyer?'

He looked startled by the suggestion and a little offended. 'No, Mrs Romanelli, I own the Heyer Gallery—London, New York and Barcelona…'

'I've heard of that.'

'You know, then, about our upcoming exhibition?'

'Not really.'

'I'm getting the feeling that you don't know that your husband brought your portfolio to us.'

Erin responded with a noncommittal smile. It was news to her that she had a…what had he said? *Portfolio?*

'Well, obviously normally we do not consider work by someone who just walks in through the door, but your husband, he…'

'Doesn't take no for an answer?'

'Forceful.'

More a force of nature, Erin thought, wondering what Francesco had done to make this man look as though he were recalling a fight with a grizzly with toothache.

'Your husband is also a very difficult man to negotiate with—I'd say you are very lucky to have him as your agent.'

I have an agent?

'He's one of a kind,' she agreed cautiously.

'Mr Romanelli mentioned you were here and I was passing so I just dropped by to tell you how *excited* we are by your work. *Really excited!* That's all I wanted to say. I hope you feel better soon.'

'Thank you.'

* * *

It was two hours later when Francesco arrived. Two hours during which Erin had totally failed to unravel the riddle of the man with the beard.

'I hear they are releasing you in the morning.'

'Finally. I had a visitor this afternoon. A Peter Heyer.'

In the act of shrugging off his jacket, Francesco paused.

'He is very excited, apparently.'

'He is, it seemed to me, quite an excitable sort of man.'

'I didn't have the faintest idea what he was talking about. I have an agent…a portfolio…?' She folded her arms across her chest. 'Do you mind telling me what is going on?'

'When I was at your studio—'

Erin, her eyes wide with amazement, cut across him. 'You were at my studio. Why would you be?'

'I was getting some things you asked for from your flat when I came across this very nice lady. She wanted the photos you did of her daughter's wedding. She was, incidentally, most pleased with the results.

'While I was there I came across some of your work…not the photographs which people pay you to take, not that they are not very competent.'

Erin knew he was talking about the boxes stacked from floor to ceiling in a cupboard.

'They're just for me. I've been snapping things since I was in my teens. I know it's digital age and everything, but I—'

'It is a criminal waste to hide away such works of art in a cupboard,' he reproached her. 'They are quite remarkable, Erin.'

'You think so?' His admiration gave her a warm feeling.

'I do and I am not the only one. I was aware that Heyers have an upcoming exhibition at the end of the year showcasing new female talent right across the art spectrum. I took a selection of your work.'

'I would never have had the guts to do that.'

'I would never have had the talent to compose a picture that sets it apart. That makes it the one that people look at in a room of twenty others. And please resist the temptation to say something self-deprecating and humble,' he continued. 'You are good and it isn't just my opinion. You heard what the man said…they are very excited. They clearly think that you are going to be the star of the show.'

Erin regarded him with a shaken fascination. 'You really did that? For me?' She couldn't recall another time in her life when anyone had shown such faith in her ability, or for that matter as much interest!

At home her habit of walking around with a camera slung around her neck had been considered mildly eccentric. Her decision to make it her living had not gone down well at all. Her parents had not given up hope she would one day get a proper job.

One more suited to a woman.

'All I did was show it to the right people.' He dismissed his contribution with a shrug. 'Your work deserves to be seen,' he said as he walked over to the chessboard that had been set out on a table.

'And don't forget as agent I get ten per cent of everything you make so it is in my best interests to make sure you become a success.'

'You really think people will buy my pictures?' The idea still seemed vaguely surreal to Erin.

'In their hordes, I shouldn't wonder.' He paused. 'I was speaking to your doctor earlier…'

Her hand went to her stomach. 'What about? There's nothing wrong, is there?'

'Quite the opposite. He's extremely pleased with your

progress and he sees no reason for us to delay our flight to Italy. We could go directly there tomorrow after they discharge you.'

She swallowed. 'I didn't expect that,' she admitted.

'Well, the alternative would seem to be for you to stay with your mother and I somehow can't see her in the role of nurse.'

'I don't need a nurse.'

'No, but you need someone who will restrain your impulses to overexert yourself. I was thinking when we interview for the nanny maybe it would be an idea to make some enquiries about a maternity nurse at the same time. I understand that they move in for the last weeks of the pregnancy, as well, obviously, as afterwards.'

'Will she have the baby for me, too?'

Baffled by the sarcasm in her voice and the annoyance in the eyes raised to his, Francesco shook his head. 'Is there a problem?'

'When did I say I wanted a nanny?'

'Well, obviously I assumed—'

She lifted her chin. 'Well, you assumed wrong. I don't want a nanny and as for a maternity nurse—it's a stupid idea.'

'You're being totally irrational.'

'If you even *whisper* the word hormone I'll strangle you,' she promised. 'There is nothing irrational about not wanting to farm your kid off to someone else.'

'A nanny isn't there to replace you, she's there to free up your time so that you can do other things.'

'What—like pander to your needs? Millions of other women cope without a nanny and so will I.'

'What if you're too exhausted by being awake nights to enjoy your baby?' He read the total intransigence in her face and threw up his hands in a very Latin gesture of exasperation. 'You'll change your mind in the end.'

She swallowed her irritation at the smug prediction. She didn't want to argue. A few days ago she had feared she was going to lose their baby—it seemed ridiculous to be squabbling now about something that, in the great scheme of things, was not terribly important.

'Maybe you're right—maybe I will change my mind,' she said, thinking, *In a pig's eye!* While she was prepared to stand her ground there was no point being confrontational now.

Francesco, not knowing that her *maybe* was of the when-hell-freezes-over variety, nodded his head in approval. 'Well, it's early days.'

'Yes, it is,' she agreed.

'My parents are very anxious to finally meet you.'

'How is your mother?'

'She spends a lot of time at Rafe's grave. It's hard,' he admitted, 'to know whether that is a good thing or not.'

'The flowers she sent were beautiful and the phone call was very sweet. She must be anxious to see you.'

She looked at her belly. It was difficult to imagine that one day her baby would grow up and leave her.

'Over the moon since she heard the news about the baby. As for seeing me, I think there is a little of the double-edged sword about that.'

Erin gave a baffled frown. 'How do you mean?'

'She cannot see me without being reminded of Rafe.'

Just as he was every time he caught sight of himself in a mirror! Not that Erin imagined for a second that he needed any reminder. She suspected that he would feel the loss of his twin for the rest of his life.

'It's strange. If Rafe hadn't died, you wouldn't be sitting

here with me now. And—' she looked down and gently massaged the gentle mound of her belly, which over the past week had become too pronounced to be hidden by loose clothes, '—there would be no baby.'

'We might have met anyway,' he suggested.

'Possibly,' she conceded. 'But we'd never have married. The circumstances would have been different.'

You would have been different, she thought, looking at him. *You wouldn't have had a gaping big hole to fill.*

'A bit like that film…have you seen it? I forget the name. It's all about one pivotal decision. You take one path and it's happy ever after. You take the other and…' She mimed a slashing motion across her throat.

As happy-ever-after paths did not usually include divorce and emergency surgery, Francesco assumed she considered she thought she had taken the latter.

'Well, we are not living in a film, *cara*. We are living in the real world, a world where you are married to me, and I am the father of your child.'

The severity of his clipped delivery caused her smooth brow to furrow in bewilderment.

'So you will just have to put your personal feelings about me to one side.'

This suggestion drew a shaky laugh from her. 'God, but I wish it was that easy.' That easy to stop loving him so much it hurt.

When Erin glanced up from her brooding contemplation of her interlocked fingers she was startled by the suppressed pain in his face.

She didn't have the faintest idea what she could have done or said to put it there, though she had no doubt if it hadn't been for her invalid status he would have quickly told her!

Francesco stayed for a little longer and explained about the travel arrangements for the following day, but the easy intimacy of earlier had vanished.

When he left he didn't kiss her.

For the first time she was actually grateful that she was on bedrest because it meant that there was no chance of her acting on her compulsion to run after him. An act she would undoubtedly have regretted later.

CHAPTER THIRTEEN

ERIN woke, her body bathed in sweat.

She lay there waiting for her heart rate to slow, the images from the repetitive nightmare still vivid in her mind. She turned her head and glanced at the clock. It was just after one.

With a groan she lifted herself on her elbow and punched the pillow.

Clutching it to her chest, she turned over. 'It'll be better when I'm out of here,' she told herself.

'Hospital beds are notoriously uncomfortable.'

A small fractured cry left her lips as the shadowy figure in the chair rose.

'What are you doing here? It's the middle of the night.' Erin experienced the confusing rush of emotions that she always did when she saw him.

If a nurse came to take her pulse at that moment Erin knew her chances of going home the next day would be nil! It was far more likely that she would find herself rushed to Intensive Care and put on life support!

His long lashes fell in a screen against the angle of his cheekbones as he stretched and dragged both hands through his hair. 'I was passing.'

He did not mention that he had been passing last night, too.

What the night staff made of a man who came to watch his wife sleep he could not imagine!

'*Passing…?*' She reached for the light cord above her head and blinked as the beam of the reading lamp fell directly on her face.

'I didn't mean to wake you.'

'Look, I know what this is about.'

Francesco went very still, colour seeping into his face consolidating into two dark bands of colour along the slashing angle of his cheekbones.

Frowning, she absently toyed with the shoestring strap of her nightgown and gave a shamed sigh.

'I'm not stupid, Francesco. I mean, you've been haunting the place. It's obvious you think that I'm going to do something stupid the moment your back is turned. Though quite what you think I'm going to do in a hospital bed, I don't know.

'But don't worry, I've learnt my lesson. From now on,' she promised him, curving a protective hand over her stomach, 'I will always put the baby first. I will treat every stair with caution.'

She saw some of the tension slip from his shoulders and assumed that she had succeeded in reassuring him.

'Have you finished?'

'I don't blame you for thinking me an unfit mother—I do myself.'

Francesco cursed softly in his own tongue.

Startled by the outrage in his expression, Erin sat passively as he strode across the room and framed her heart-shaped face between his big hands.

Her skin prickled with heat at his touch.

He studied her upturned features, the pallor only relieved by a light flush across the crests of her smooth cheekbones.

Francesco found himself longing to erase the haunted shadows from her lovely eyes. 'You are not an unfit mother!'

Francesco closed his eyes and cursed. 'What happened was not your fault. The sooner the better you are out of this place. Part of the problem is you have far too much time to think.'

'You make it sound like thinking is a bad thing.'

Perhaps there was something in what he said? It was difficult to keep things in proportion when you woke in the middle of the night sure that your baby was dead.

'You were the one who said that I needed someone to restrain my impulses!' she reminded him.

Francesco, who couldn't recall saying anything similar, dredged his memory. 'What I actually said was restrain your impulses to overexert yourself, which was my way of saying you needed looking after without you going feral on me, which you are prone to do at the merest *hint* that you might not be totally self-sufficient.'

He traced the curve of her cheek with his thumb.

'You have to let go of your fear,' he said softly. 'If our baby had died it would have been a tragedy, but he didn't and it wasn't.'

'But you blame me...'

'I blame me!' he blurted out.

A look of total bewilderment crossed her face. 'You?' she echoed. 'Why should you feel blame?'

'Why?' He stared down at her incredulously. 'How can you ask that? If I had not put you in a position where you felt you had to run away from me the accident would never have happened. If you or the baby had been harmed it would have been my fault.'

'That's the craziest logic I've ever heard. It was an accident. I tripped...' She suddenly laughed as the irony hit. 'My God,

I've been lying here thinking you're blaming me and you've been blaming yourself... You know, it's actually quite funny when you think about it.'

Francesco's expression did not suggest he saw the funny side. 'I don't seem to be able to stop the people I care for getting hurt.'

People...? Things suddenly slipped into place. *So that was it!*

'I fell, Francesco. You didn't push me, the same way you didn't make Rafe take his life.'

Erin heard the sibilant hiss of his sharp intake of breath. His head came up and his dark eyes locked with hers.

'Some things in life even *you* don't have any control over,' she told him softly. 'I know that's pretty hard for a control freak like yourself to accept,' she teased gently, 'but...'

'You think you know me so well.'

The smile faded from her face. 'Sometimes I don't think I know you at all,' she admitted huskily as she looked at the enigma who was her husband.

'I'm an open book.'

This claim made Erin laugh. 'You're the most compli-cated, contradictory man I've ever met.'

'After twenty years of marriage you'll find me boring and predictable.'

'Do you think we'll still be together in twenty years?'

Her unthinking exclamation shattered the intimacy of the moment. 'You are thinking in the short term?'

'Well, it seems a good idea to take things one day at a time.'

His expression was remote and forbidding; it was clear her response was not one he liked. Francesco picked up his jacket from the back of a chair and nodded in her general direction.

'You need your sleep.'

She was suddenly loath to see him walk out of the door.

What if he never comes back? The irrational thought just popped into her head and she said the first thing that came into her head—unfortunately it concerned milky drinks.

'I could ask the nurse to get us a drink of cocoa, or something else if you prefer.'

'Cocoa?'

The mortified colour rushed to her cheeks.

She had never felt more ridiculous in her life. Francesco could hardly be unfamiliar with women who offered him inducements to stay around, but she would have bet none of them had ever tried to entice him with a cup of cocoa!

'Good night, Erin.'

Erin had arrived at the hospital in an ambulance. She left in a helicopter.

They flew straight to the airport where they waited in the VIP lounge.

Erin did not have much time to avail herself of the facilities before it was time for them to board the Romanelli private jet.

It all felt surreal to Erin. She suspected she ought to be feeling more outrage at the extravagance. She actually had a sneaking suspicion it would be disturbingly easy to get used to this sort of luxury.

'I feel like royalty or a Hollywood star or something,' she said, pushing her leather seat into full recline position and spinning around.

Francesco watched her with an indulgent smile. 'You'll make yourself dizzy.'

Erin, who was already dizzy, stopped spinning. It occurred to her that he must be contrasting her childish antic unfavourably with those of his worldly friends.

'I wonder if I'll ever be able to do a convincing sophisticated?'

'If by sophisticated you mean artificial, I sincerely hope not.'

She leaned forward and planted her elbows on the table that was between them. 'I suppose I mean elegant.'

'Elegance is good, but then so is spontaneity and enthusiasm.'

She levelled a finger at her chest. 'Me?'

'Definitely you.'

'I'd prefer to look like Audrey Hepburn.'

Francesco laughed.

'It probably makes me very shallow, but having sampled it I've decided this is the only way to travel,' she confessed guiltily.

'Have I said…you look very beautiful today?'

She slid a not quite steady hand down the bodice of her sleeveless dress. The deceptively modest rounded neckline was cut low enough to reveal the upper curves of her breasts, which was probably why it had sat in her wardrobe unworn. The bias-cut skirt of soft voile fitted nicely over her small bump and flared around her calves clinging to her legs as she moved.

The duck-blue colour did good things for her eyes and made her skin look translucently pale. Against the bare skin of her shoulders her hair stood out like a flame. The effect was dramatic and feminine.

'It isn't what I would have chosen,' she admitted.

But she hadn't chosen it, Francesco had. Considering the things that were packed in her case, she wondered if he had even looked at the list she had given him!

Wearing this dress was like hanging a sign around her neck saying 'I'm available,' with a subheading of 'Take me please!'

'You are inclined to hide your light, *cara*. What do they say? If you have it, flaunt it?'

'I just don't think that it is necessary to wave it in their faces and jump up and down saying look at me, as well.'

At that moment the young attendant, casually dressed,

like the rest of the crew, in jeans and a shirt, made her for-
tuitous arrival.

Erin declined food but said she would love a cup of tea.
Francesco overruled her with a display of high-handedness
that was typical of him and said she would have something
light, scrambled egg with a little smoked salmon perhaps?

Despite Erin's insistence that she couldn't eat a thing, the
light dish was actually so delicious she polished off the lot and
had a second cup of tea.

They were half an hour into their journey, and Francesco,
who had been to talk to the pilot, had again taken the seat
opposite her when she finally mentioned the previous night.

'At the risk of breaking the mood, about last night…' Erin
skimmed a slightly nervous look at him through the filigree
mesh of her lashes.

'You discovered I have no liking for cocoa.'

'I didn't want you to go.'

It was an admission a short time ago she would not have
made, but some time over the past days her defences had
lowered. It was about trust. Without even realising what was
happening she had started to trust him…trust her own judge-
ment. Startled by this discovery, she felt her throat thicken
with emotional tears.

Francesco, who had stilled at the husky admission, released
a long sibilant sigh. 'I didn't particularly want to go myself.'

Her startled eyes flew to his. 'You didn't?'

He shook his head. 'But you were exhausted and—'

'I don't like falling asleep. Since the accident I have been
having these nightmares…I wake up convinced that the
baby has died.'

Francesco gave a horrified exclamation in Italian. Out of
his seat in a heartbeat, he dropped on his knees beside her seat

and took her small hands between his. 'Your hands are cold,' he said, drawing them to his mouth and kissing each palm before enfolding them once more in his warm strong grip. 'Why didn't you say something about the nightmares?' he reproached thickly.

Shoulders hunched, she gave a jerky little shrug. 'I was being stupid, I know that. It was just a dream…the same one each time.' She swallowed. 'About the baby, and I know it's stupid because even *you* can't do much about dreams, but if I'd known you were there I wouldn't have felt so afraid of falling asleep. I suppose I feel safe with you around.'

Francesco sucked in a deep breath; the strong angles of his lean face seemed carved of stone as he stared at her.

Lost in his eyes, Erin hardly noticed that the silence between them had stretched into minutes.

When he did speak Francesco's accent was perceptibly thicker than normal. 'You don't have to be afraid of falling asleep again because I will be there.' With a slow smile that made her stomach flip, he leaned across and cupped her chin in his hand. 'And I will be there when you wake up, too.'

Beneath the sweep of his lashes she could see the dark liquid glow of his eyes as they moved across her face. He was so close she could feel the warmth of his breath on her cheek. In her chest her heart started to thud slow and hard, banging as if it were making an escape attempt against her ribcage.

'I would really like to kiss you,' he said thickly.

The heat in his liquid eyes as they lingered on her mouth made her dizzy. She was drowning in a warm, languid lethargy that made her throat dry and her limbs heavy and that was drawing her thoughts dangerously towards the idea of dropping her defences completely and telling him how she really felt.

When his lips, warm and firm, touched her own a deep sigh

that was almost relief shuddered through her body. Under the skilful pressure of his mouth her lips parted.

When Francesco lifted his head she gave a soft, throaty murmur of protest.

He ran a brown finger slowly along the soft curve of her cheek and closed his eyes before pressing a long, languid kiss on her parted lips. 'I love your mouth,' he slurred.

And I love you, she thought, and felt the salty moisture leak out from under her sealed eyelids.

'I think…' she said, trying to ease herself away from him even though every fibre in her body was reluctant to break the contact. 'I think we should…'

'Of course.'

The speed and apparent ease with which he disentangled himself on a physical and mental level astonished Erin, whose body was still humming with desire.

She felt the stirrings of resentment as he returned to his seat. He searched her face, the groove above his masterful nose deepening.

'What's wrong?'

'I was just wishing that I could turn it on and off the way you apparently can.'

She saw a look of comprehension spread across his face. 'You did ask me to stop.'

'I know…I know I'm being unreasonable, but you could have pretended it was difficult.'

'I wouldn't have been pretending.'

'But…'

'I didn't think I had to spell out what you do to me, Erin, but I can if you like.'

Erin swallowed as the liquid warmth in the pit of her stomach pooled hotly. 'I'll pass,' she gritted huskily.

'You never used to be so prissy. Why are you uncomfortable talking about sex? Your candour used to be quite a turn-on.'

She maintained eye contact, but it took every ounce of self-control she had to do so. The tide of warm colour rising up her neck she could do nothing about.

'I'm fine talking about sex.' Though from his previous observations clearly she had lost her edge when it came to doing it! 'I'm just not obsessed with the subject like you.'

He gave a grin that was sinfully attractive as he ran a hand along his jaw. 'I must shave before we land. You are adorable.'

Hearing the raw, driven note in this disconnected addition made her study him more closely. She immediately saw that he was not nearly as composed as she had first supposed.

She watched the nerve that ticked away like a time bomb in his sexily hollow cheek and was glad that she wasn't the only one suffering.

'Dio!' he groaned, letting his head fall back and sighing. 'You always were the best sex ever.'

It was remarkable how one slurred comment could totally obliterate the warm romantic glow. What had seemed unique and beautiful now felt crude and coarse.

I suppose, she reflected grimly, *I ought to be grateful that he didn't pretend to feel something that he clearly didn't.*

Erin lifted her chin and smiled. 'It's always gratifying to be told you're the best sex someone has ever had.'

He lifted his head and surveyed her smiling face with bafflement.

Erin could see why he might be confused. Tell the average male that he was the best sex you'd ever had and he would be preening himself, say the self-same thing to most women and they would be insulted, though it did kind of depend on the setting. There were some situations where she could imagine not finding such a comment tacky at all.

'Have I done something wrong?'

'Not a thing.'

Her gaze swivelled to his; the intense blue hit him just as strongly now as it had done the very first time he had seen her.

Francesco stretched his long legs out in front of him and crossed one foot over the other.

Erin was almost as surprised as Francesco appeared to be to hear herself say, 'I should have told you about the baby.'

'We don't need to talk about that now.'

'I need to. I knew I ought to have told you straight away, but I was kind of in shock…and…' she closed her eyes '…I know you think I was a quitter to walk away from our marriage. I know you think that I took the easy way out, but it *wasn't*…'

'Wasn't?' He studied her downcast features with a frown. 'I don't understand what you're saying, Erin.'

She shook her head, her luminous eyes starting to feel tired as she looked at him. 'No,' she agreed, 'you *don't see* at all. Walking away wasn't *easy*, it was the *hardest* thing I have ever done in my life,' she told him in a voice that shook with the strength of her feelings. 'It…' she swallowed and expelled a long shaky sigh '…it was painful,' she explained with admirable understatement. 'If I had to do it again I'd…I simply don't think I could bear it.'

Francesco's expression was stunned as Erin absently dabbed the back of her hand to her cheek to blot a tear running down her face. 'You won't need to. We will make it work,' he promised thickly.

She expelled a deep gusty sigh. 'We don't really have much choice, do we?' she said, struggling to sound pragmatic.

'Did you ever consider raising the baby alone?'

The question drew a shaky laugh from her.

'What,' he asked, looking considerably taken aback by her response, 'is so funny?'

'I suppose the big worry for some women in my situation might have been whether the father would want to know, or if he would question the baby was his. That was never my problem. Don't you think, Francesco, that I haven't always known that there was no way you'd allow your child…a Romanelli…to be brought up without his father?'

'But of course a child should be brought up with two parents within the safety of—'

Shaking her head, Erin cut across him. 'Any child would be a hell of a lot better brought up in a single-parent situation than in a home where the parents have a relationship based on lies and deceit. Believe me, I know…oh, God.' She covered her mouth with both hands. 'My parents' marriage has really messed me up, hasn't it?'

'Was it very bad?'

Erin looked at him, gave a twisted little smile that just about broke his heart, and then with a faraway look in her eyes began to recount a story.

'I was walking to school one day and I saw my father, which was strange because he had promised me the night before that he would bring me back a nice present from his trip to York. Anyway, there he was standing on the doorstep of a house not half a mile from ours kissing a blonde. Half my class saw him, too—kids are not kind,' she said with massive understatement.

Francesco growled a violent epithet in his own tongue.

'How old were you?'

'About six or seven, I should think.'

He shook his head, his face creased in a grimace of disgust. '*Dio*! Did you tell your mother?'

'I did. She got hysterical; my father was there. There was a lot of shouting and he packed a bag and walked out. Mum turned to me and screamed, "Look what you've done!"'

'I thought it was my fault. I didn't realise until much later that she already knew. She always had known; she had chosen to turn a blind eye.'

Francesco would have done anything in that moment to assuage the pain he saw in her eyes. He would also have liked to throttle the selfish couple who had used her like a bit-part player in the long-running soap that was their marriage.

He might have to tolerate them because he was married to their daughter, but he was determined that he would let them know his feelings on the subject. And let them know also that he would no longer tolerate the situation.

'I suppose you could say that I was conditioned from an early age to expect men to cheat.'

'People make mistakes.'

Puzzled by the odd intensity of his gaze, she nodded. 'Sure they do; it's part of being human.'

'If they are genuinely sorry and regret that mistake, should they not be given a second chance?'

The colour seeped from her face. 'Was that a confession?' she asked.

'*I* have nothing to confess to.'

Shocked by the discovery that she believed him Erin expelled a long, shaky sigh.

'I know.' The relief of being freed from all those doubts was incredible. If Francesco ever cheated he would tell her. He just wasn't a sneak-around sort of guy.

'What did you say?'

'I said that I believe you.'

Francesco searched her face. What he saw there caused his shoulder to relax. Their eyes clung until finally he nodded.

'Thank you,' she said, heaving a sigh of relief. 'God, you must think I'm a real head case.'

When he finally spoke his voice was pitched seductively low and his accent was more strongly defined than usual. 'No, I don't think that. I think you are a perfect fit. I would call you a perfect fit.'

Erin drew a shuddery breath as images conjured by his throaty words floated through her head of sweat-coated bodies intimately entwined. As the heat flooded through her body she closed her eyes and thought about him hard inside her, moving. She gritted her teeth and ejected the image forcibly from her mind.

When she opened her eyes he was still looking at her, his expression only marginally less seductive than his velvet-toned voice had been—if ever a man had been given a voice designed for making indecent suggestions it was Francesco, she reflected with an inward sigh.

She tried to inject a note of levity to lower the tension. 'How many times have you used that line?'

'You seem to find the truth difficult to cope with, Erin.'

'You wouldn't recognise the truth if it bit you,' she snapped back crankily.

'The only person who has ever bitten me is you, *cara*.' His laugh deepened as the colour flew to her cheeks. 'You remember the occasion, too, I see.'

'Dear God, no wonder we never get to work through our issues. It always ends up with us trying to rip each other's clothes off.'

'You say that as though it is a problem. And I have no issues.'

She regarded him with frustration. 'That sort of attitude is why we… Don't you realise that our marriage has been based on a tissue of lies. Oh, I know lies of omission for the most part, but it amounts to the same thing.

'First you don't tell me who you really are, then you don't even mention Rafe…' She saw Francesco stiffen at the mention of his brother's name.

'I can see why you didn't tell me about him,' she admitted. 'But when you marry someone you can't be selective about what you tell them and what you don't. I know that I have my own issues, but can't you see that knowing you have no problem lying to me when it suits you makes it hard for me to believe you when something happens…and, well…I think I've said enough.'

And none of it, she suspected, had been very lucid, but she just hoped she had got her point across.

'So,' he said slowly, 'what you want off me is honesty and straight-talking?'

What I want off you is love. Her eyes fell from his. 'It would be a start.'

'That,' he conceded, 'does not seem an excessive request.' He arched a brow. 'If I don't deliver on your demands…?'

She was about to say that they weren't really demands when the plane dropped like a stone for what felt like several thousand feet, but had been, she later learned, less. Erin screamed, and grabbed the side of her chair.

We're going to die! I'll never get the chance to see my baby. Never get the chance to lie next to Francesco and feel the friction of his skin against my skin, smell the warm scent of his body and enjoy the touch of his lips on my skin, taste him…

'Erin, it's fine, we'll be fine.'

She opened her eyes and found that the plane had levelled

off and during the interminable time that it had been bounced around like a cork in a stream, somehow, even though it seemed a physical impossibility, Francesco had moved around to her side of the table.

She presumed that the arm resembling a steel bar that was clamped across her was the reason she had not been thrown from her seat.

A voice, presumably the pilot, came over the loud-speaker system. 'Mr Romanelli, would you like to come up front? There could be a bit more of that.'

'What does he think you can do about it?' she demanded indignantly.

'An extra pair of hands on these occasions does not come amiss,' Francesco said, strapping her into her seat and giving a thumbs-up sign to the shaken-looking female attendant who was strapping herself into the seat beside her. Erin would have thought that any pilot would have wanted to keep non-essential people clear of the cockpit on such occasions, but she kept this opinion to herself.

When he bent down to brush his lips against hers and promised that there was no need to worry, she saw the gleam of exhilaration in his eyes and realised that, far from being terrified, her husband was enjoying this.

It wasn't the best time in the world to learn you had married a madman, the sort of crazy who got a kick out of situations that would turn normal people into quivering lumps of jelly.

Her expression was indignant as she watched him stride away. 'I don't see why they want him. It's not as if he'd be much use if the copilot falls out of the window or something.'

'Well, actually,' said the girl beside her, 'he would. He's licensed to fly this baby.'

'Francesco has a pilot's licence?'

She could see the girl thought it a bit odd that his wife wouldn't have this piece of information, but she was too polite to say so.

'He flies himself occasionally.'

Erin was spared the need to respond because they encountered some more turbulence. She never did ask Francesco if he had been in control while they endured the next ten minutes.

He finally joined her as they were circling the airport. He studied her face with concern.

'You look shattered.'

'You don't.' Obviously cheating death at twenty thousand feet was something that he found relaxing. 'Guess which one of us is the normal one?'

He grinned and said she could nap on the drive out of the city.

CHAPTER FOURTEEN

AND Erin did just that. She slept most of the way from the airport and woke as they turned onto the last mile of track that led to the home she had once shared with Francesco.

She felt her excitement mount as she picked out familiar landmarks.

'You've resurfaced the road.'

He nodded. 'I think you'll find I have made quite a few changes.'

The location hadn't changed—it was still simply stunning. It enjoyed total privacy, and mouth-watering far-reaching views over the hills and forests of the estate and beyond.

'You've been doing some landscaping,' she began, assuming the cleared section filled now with rows of olive tress were the changes he had referred to, when the house came into view and she knew she'd been wrong.

She caught her breath.

No matter what your taste architecturally, Erin doubted anyone arriving here would not gasp.

'You've finished it!'

He pulled up on the cobbled area in front of the building and nodded. He held out his hands palm up for her inspection. 'How do you think I got these?' he asked, revealing a set of workmanlike calluses, which she duly admired.

Head tilted back to get the full effect of the structure as she got out of the car, she shook her head in silent wonder as she walked towards the building.

Placing her hand palm flat against the ancient stone wall, which looked solid enough to withstand just about anything you threw at it including the odd earthquake, she turned back to Francesco.

'This is incredible—when did it happen?' Without waiting for his response, she stepped back to admire once more the stunning building.

The two wings of the house were now connected. The glass corridor linking them looked exactly as Francesco had described. A glass gable end stood where there had once been rubble.

'I don't know what to say, Francesco. It's magnificent. I'm breathless.'

'So am I. You're beautiful.'

Erin spun around, her eyes colliding with his. She shivered in response to the raw heat in his midnight eyes.

'So you like what I have done?'

She nodded, feeling suddenly and inexplicably shy. 'I love it. When did...?'

'I was at something of a loose end when you left. I could not work.'

'You couldn't work?'

'Perhaps I should have said didn't want to work. A list of figures no longer provided me with the fulfilment it once had, Actually I was pretty much a wreck,' he confessed wryly.

Looking at his lean and lithe body, it was hard to think of Francesco and wreck in the same sentence. The shock revelations continued to come thick and fast.

'Once I sobered up...'

'You got *drunk*?'

'It was the bender to end all benders. I discovered that I am not an interesting drunk so I sobered up.' He paused and angled an enquiring look at her face. 'I know you wanted honesty and openness, but is this too much information?'

Erin laughed. 'Is that what this is about?'

The laughter died from his face.

'This is about being someone you believe will love and care for you and our baby for the rest of your life. You shared your thoughts and feelings with me. I am simply returning the compliment.'

There were several thoughts and feelings that she had not been brave enough to share with him.

Erin knew the message in his dark eyes wasn't really there. She knew her brain was playing cruel tricks, making her see what she wanted to.

But what if it was really there? Her heart began to beat faster.

'Now where had I got to? Of course, I was filling in the gaps—it was at that point, I realised that the biggest favour I could do to the bank was to stay away.'

'Can you do that?'

He gave one of his inimitable shrugs. 'I'm the boss, *cara*. I can do anything I like and,' he admitted, his lips curling into a sardonic smile, 'I am very good at delegating. I hope you understand that during this time I was very angry with you.'

'What did you do next, other than be angry with me?'

'I came back here and I thought when Erin comes back our home will be finished.'

'You thought I would come back?'

'I could not allow myself to think anything else,' he said simply. 'That night in Venice, the night of the ball, your obvious distrust of me, the things you accused me of—I cannot lie, I was very, *very* angry. My pride was hurt...I walked... God knows where. I knew if I came back I would say things that I would regret.

'And part of me, a not very nice part of me, took pleasure from the possibility you might think I was with another woman. It was petty and contemptible.' He looked with pained anguish into her blue eyes. 'But my plan backfired. When I came back to find you leaving me I was shocked. I think I was *in* shock.

'I didn't really think you would do it. My pride would not let me believe that a woman would reject Francesco Romanelli.' He gave a snort of self-derision at his arrogance. 'But you did. I let you go. I can't believe how stupid I was!' he admitted with a groan. 'I actually sat and watched while you, my one chance of happiness, walked out of my life.'

Is he talking about me? Am I his one chance at happiness?

'After you had gone I just sat there on the bed expecting that you would walk in any moment.

'It was a crushing blow when you didn't and...well, I have told you how I spent our time apart.'

'That night in Venice, when I went back to the room I recognised even then that my jealousy was the cause of the problem. I planned to discuss it with you, but when the minutes ticked by, well...it felt that something was dying inside me.' She gave a great gulp and covered her mouth with her hand. 'I thought you didn't care,' she admitted, her voice cracking. 'That I'd pushed you into another woman's arms.'

With a cry, Francesco reached for her own hand resting in the hollow of her back, the other cradling the back of her head. 'I felt the same way,' he admitted, brushing her hair back from her brow and raining reverent kisses on the smooth skin he had exposed.

'But if I had trusted you, if I hadn't let my wretched imagination go wild…we would never…'

He silenced her protest with a kiss so achingly tender that it brought fresh tears to Erin's eyes. With a sigh she sagged against him, her face pressed into his chest while he murmured soft endearments and kissed her hair. It was some time later that they moved by mutual consent towards the big metal-studded door.

'I hope you'll approve of what I've done to our home, Erin.'

Her ability to think straight blasted into oblivion by the amazing things he had just said, she nodded. Her legs felt so weak with reaction to the revelations of the last few minutes that she needed the support of the hand in the small of her back that guided her towards the massive front door.

'You know how you said a baby grand would look good in the summer sitting room when it had a roof?'

She tilted an enquiring look up at him.

'Well, it now has a roof and a baby grand.'

She was laughing when she walked through the door. She was laughing all the way up to the point someone screamed 'Surprise!' and what seemed like hundreds of people leapt out laughing and shouting and in some cases waving banners.

'*Dio mio*…!' Francesco gritted through clenched teeth as he pulled her into his side. 'I swear to you, *cara* I had no idea. If I had I would have hired stunt doubles for the occasion.'

'Don't scowl,' she said, sticking a warning elbow in his side and hiding her own dismay and frustration behind a smile. 'They're trying to be nice.'

'Best not to mention the rough flight to my mother,' Francesco said as a middle-aged couple approached.

Looking curiously at the distinguished-looking man with the mane of white hair, Erin knew exactly what her husband would look like in thirty years' time. The woman with the gentle eyes and a sweet smile was leaning lightly on a cane. There were tears in her eyes as she embraced first Erin and then Francesco.

'At last we meet. She is so lovely, Francesco, and that hair…we are so happy about the baby.'

'I want you both to know,' Alberto said, clapping his son warmly on the shoulder, 'that *this* was not my idea.' His grimace took in the entire heaving room. 'If anyone ever thinks about doing this to me…'

'Do not be tiresome, Alberto,' recommended Sabina Romanelli. 'Livia thought it would be nice for Erin to meet the family.'

'Because she got out of hospital and it would be so restful,' said Francesco at his most sardonic.

'I think it's a lovely idea,' Erin said.

'You're lying through your lovely teeth, but, if that's the way you want to play it, fine—I'm throwing you to the wolves. I warn you, Erin, not everyone survives the Romanelli initiation ritual. She thinks I'm joking,' he said to his father.

'They'll suck you dry and spit you out,' the elder Romanelli said straight-faced.

It was easy to see where Francesco got his sense of humour from.

'Good luck, *cara*!' Francesco whispered in her ear the moment before she was whisked away.

It was a good hour later before she saw Francesco again. The smile of welcome on her face faded when she saw his expression.

'What,' he demanded, 'do you think you're doing?'

'Doing?' Erin said, mystified by his attitude. 'I'm not doing anything.'

He shook his dark head in disbelief. 'You really are unbelievable,' he said, forcibly removing the fretful toddler she was jiggling on one hip from her arms. 'You had surgery a few days ago and you're pregnant. Lugging a little monster like this around is not what I'd call *lots of rest and relaxation*.'

'He's not heavy,' Erin protested.

'Yes, he is, and he is also,' Francesco discovered, angling a critical look at the toddler's face, 'extremely dirty. I'm taking him back to his mother.'

'You know, I think I've had enough of this, and you,' he added, glancing at her face, 'have definitely had enough.'

'What are you doing, Francesco?' she asked as he began to bang his hand on the table.

'I'm getting rid of this lot.'

'You can't do that!' she protested. 'It would be incredibly rude.'

Actually Francesco was rude and charming in equal parts as he basically told his family they had outstayed their welcome and fortunately nobody seemed particularly offended.

CHAPTER FIFTEEN

By the time the last of their party-throwers had taken their leave Erin couldn't help but be glad that Francesco had taken direct action.

She still couldn't believe that—after all her fears that she would struggle to adapt to a world so far removed from the one she knew, and that his family would think he had married beneath him—in the end they had gathered her to their collective bosom unreservedly. The thing she would always remember about today would be the incredible warmth of her welcome.

Her head was filled with faces and buzzing with names. It was small wonder that she had the beginnings of a headache.

Francesco had not been exaggerating when he'd said he had a large family.

During the party Erin's thoughts had repeatedly returned to the moments in the garden before they had walked into their surprise party. She had kept thinking about the things he had said and the expression in his eyes. It had made it hard for her to concentrate on what people had been saying to her and being forced to wait to hear what else he had to say had been incredibly frustrating.

So many questions still remained unanswered. She had

felt so optimistic, so confident when they had walked through the door. But things had been left hanging in the air and during the frustrating delay doubts had crept in.

Maybe he didn't even realise yet, but one thing was perfectly plain to Erin; Francesco hadn't been in love with her when he'd married her. In lust, yes, but not in love.

She had been a diversion. If he had been kissing her he hadn't been thinking about his brother. Was it possible that he had really fallen in love with her since they had married? Or was she succumbing to that most common of human failings and seeing only what she wanted to? Wasn't it more likely that his new warmth and tenderness had more to do with the fact she was the mother of his unborn child and he wanted their marriage to work?

A moment later Francesco walked into the room massaging the back of his neck. 'I've pulled up the drawbridge.'

And by the expression in her eyes as she looked at him it looked as if Erin had, too. He silently cursed his family's timing. Things had been going in exactly the right direction until they had been ambushed.

'And this is the family you thought you were not sophisticated enough to be part of,' he said, removing a paper streamer from around his neck. 'They like you.'

'And I like them.'

'The question is do you like me, Erin?'

'You know I do, despite the fact you give orders and you issue decrees, you ride roughshod over people's feelings and you think you're always right!'

'Is there more? Because I warn you my ego is feeling pretty fragile right now.'

A flicker of a smile crossed her face. 'You've got an ego the size of Manchester.'

'You think I will ever find a woman willing to overlook my failings?'

Only several million.

'Are you worried you won't?'

'I wasn't,' he admitted. 'In fact, I thought I already had. But suddenly I don't sound like the template for anyone's perfect man.'

Her eyes dropped from his. 'That kind of depends on the woman,' she mumbled, thinking that for her he would always represent the perfect man.

'Erin!'

The urgency in his voice as he spoke her name drew Erin's eyes upwards.

'Just what happened...outside, I thought...' A nerve clenched in his lean cheek. 'Was I wrong?'

She shook her head. 'No...' She ran the tip of her tongue across the outline of her dry lips and lifted her chin.

Their glances locked, the tension vibrating between them like an overstrung violin string. Erin felt herself drawn in, mesmerised by the rampant hunger in the velvety depths.

The sexual inertia that started in her toes took a heartbeat to engulf her entire body. She closed her eyes, but could still see his face.

She wanted to be in his arms; he wanted her to be there.

'No...no, this is...' Breathing hard, he stepped away from her his hand held up as though to ward her off.

She reached a hand in confused protest and Francesco shook his head. 'No, when you touch me it is like throwing a flammable liquid on a smouldering fire. Not something I have a problem with, *tesora mia*,' he admitted with a strained grin. 'But right now we need to finish what we started... What we started outside before my family crashed our private party.'

Heart thudding like a hammer in her chest from a combination of anticipation and trepidation, she nodded and got to her feet. It was then she actually felt the blood slowly draining from her face; it really was the strangest sensation. She could see Francesco's lips moving, but she couldn't hear anything above the roar of the blood pounding in her ears.

Feeling strangely disconnected from what was happening, she was conscious that her knees were sagging and the floor was rushing up towards her.

The next second she found herself flat on her back on the sofa in the living room.

'If you move an inch I will kill you!'

She turned her head in the direction of this fierce threat. 'It wasn't my fault I fainted,' she protested weakly.

'Nothing is ever your fault!' he thundered. 'You are taking years off my life.'

'You look all right to me.' He looked perfect and it wasn't hard to see why other women were drawn to him.

Erin had experienced firsthand the magnetic charge of Francesco's rampant masculinity. She was pretty sure that every female with a hormone in her bloodstream got a sexual buzz just looking at him.

And mostly they wanted to do more than look, she thought. They wanted to spear their fingers into his silky dark hair and breathe in the warm male scent of his body.

Once upon a time allowing herself to think this way would have sent her into a spiral of rage and pain, but now it didn't.

Now she had total belief in his integrity.

'I love you, Francesco…' Why hadn't she said this before? 'I just wish that I'd told…'

'*Erin*…you don't have to say it. I already know.'

'I...I don't understand,' she faltered, confused by his driven, strained manner.

His deep-set eyes slid from hers. 'That day when I went looking for you...your mother, she told me...'

'Told you what?'

'We were apart for eight weeks, you were feeling vulnerable and alone. I...' A nerve along his jaw clenched as his dark eyes slid from hers. 'I really don't need to know the details.' That, he reflected grimly, would be more than he could bear. 'What matters,' he said, 'is how you feel now. And I think...I think you love me?'

It was a wary question and not an arrogant pronouncement... This was not the Francesco Erin knew.

'I do love you, Francesco,' she admitted huskily.

A hissing sigh of audible relief escaped his clamped lips. 'Then that is what matters,' he announced, his mouth firming with determination. 'Not things that...you may not think so now, Erin, but we have something very special, something which is incredibly rare. And if you are worried that I will throw this up into your face in the future, do not be.' He moved his hands in a sweep designed to illustrate that a line had been drawn under the subject. 'I swear on all that is—'

Erin, who had been listening to him with an air of bewilderment, cut across him. 'I might be more relieved if I knew what you were talking about.'

He looked pained. 'I understand, Erin—there is no need for you to lie to me.'

She could only assume that this *understanding* he claimed was responsible for the rigidity in his lean body and the nerve ticking like a time bomb in his hollow cheek.

'I'm not lying, Francesco. I have no idea what you're talking about. Please tell me what my mother told you.'

'While you were in hospital she rang me and implied that after you left me…that you, that you met someone else.'

'You think I had an affair?' The sheer absurdity of the suggestion drew a laugh from her throat.

'You don't have to pretend, Erin…'

As her thoughts raced Erin's eyes started to fill.

Seeing the sheen in the luminous depths, Francesco, misreading their cause, groaned. 'We will work through this,'

'Work through it?' she echoed.

He had been thinking that she was suffering from a guilty conscience.

And he was prepared to forgive her!

If she had ever doubted the depth of his love she didn't now. She could only imagine how hard forgiving such a lapse would be for someone with his pride.

It represented nobility of epic proportions!

'You think I had an affair and you're willing to take me back. You must love me very much?' she said in rapturous wonder.

'More than life,' he confirmed, causing more tears to leak from her eyes.

'That is so…oh, my God, Francesco, I don't deserve you,' she said in a choked voice. She took the tissue he handed her and blotted her face, smiling through the tears up at him. 'My mother was stirring…' It would be a long time, she reflected, her expression momentarily hardening as she thought of her mother, before she would forgive her for this malicious meddling.

His dark glance sharpened and flickered questioningly across her face. 'What are you telling me?'

'I'm telling you she was lying. I had no affair.' *Please let him believe me.* 'I couldn't,' she told him simply.

'You're the only man I have ever been with. The only man I've *wanted* to be with. The idea of another man touching me the way you do makes my skin crawl,' she revealed with a shudder. 'Before you I even thought I was not very highly sexed…frigid, I suppose.'

There was a long silence while he searched her face. Erin returned his gaze, her eyes glowing with her love for him, a faint smile making her soft lips quiver.

'My God…can this be true?' He sighed, a feverish shudder running through his lean body. 'I have been through such agonies,' he revealed, dragging a shaking hand through his hair. To think of another man's hands on her had made him sick to the stomach and filled him with a murderous rage the like of which he had never imagined he was capable of.

'Oh, I think I do.' Erin pulled herself into a sitting position and tucked her feet under her. 'I'm fine now,' she said quickly as Francesco opened his mouth to reproach her. 'An imagination can be a terrible thing, can't it?' she added softly.

He nodded. 'It is not something I would wish on my worst enemy. Thinking of you with…I wanted to kill him, but the worst part was the knowledge that it was my own stupid fault if you had turned to someone else. I knew how insecure your parents' relationship had made you. I should have made allowances. My God,' he breathed, coming around to sit beside her on the sofa. 'Your mother must really hate me.'

Her expression grim, Erin took his big hands between her small ones. 'My mother rarely thinks of anyone but herself.'

'But to say such a thing, it…' For a moment Francesco relived his worst nightmare. Then he took a deep sigh and closed the door firmly on those terrible images. It was a place he never wanted to visit again.

'You believe me?'

He looked indignant as he lifted her hands to his lips. 'Of course I believe you.'

Joy exploded inside her.

'If you thought I'd had an affair, did you not wonder even for a moment whether the baby…' She lowered her hand to her stomach, carrying his hand with her. 'Whether he was yours?'

Francesco curled his big hand protectively over her belly and smiled. 'Not even for a moment!'

'Well, it would be understandable if you had.'

He shook his head. 'I knew that you would never try and pass off another man's child as mine.'

His total confidence drew an emotional sob from her aching throat. 'God, you're so…' She gave a teary sniff. 'You're a much nicer person than me.'

He levelled an amused grin at her face. 'You are the only person who has ever called me nice—not even my own mother thinks I am nice.' A frown contorted his face as he asked, 'But if there was no other man, what is it that has been coming between us? You are not going to tell me that you have some stupid idea I only want you because of the baby.' His face tightened with displeasure at the thought.

'It did cross my mind, but, no, not now. It's just I knew you didn't love me when you married me.'

'I didn't love you?'

She shook her head.

'You were in a terrible place after Rafe killed himself.'

Francesco flinched at the sound of his brother's name. 'I thought we had dealt with this idea before.'

'Oh, I'm not saying you *deliberately* used me to ease the pain. But you were all over the place emotionally speaking…it was like, you know, turning up the radio to drown out the road drill.'

'I didn't turn to prescriptive drugs to dull the pain, I turned to you? Presumably you thought I would wake up one day fully healed and find you surplus to requirements.'

She nodded.

Succumbing to mirth, he threw back his head and laughed.

'You thought I was having an affair,' she pointed out when he had stopped.

'Point taken,' he conceded. 'But, *per amor di Dio*, how could you think something so crazy? Rafe's death had nothing to do with me marrying you! Except in the fact it made me appreciate that a man should grab happiness with both hands when he had it within his grasp… It is just a pity that my pride had made me lose sight of this for a while.

'Pain is part of the grieving process. I felt pain when Rafe died and I still do. I suspect I always will. While I did not embrace that pain, *cara*, I never tried to escape it.

'As for you being some sort of distraction, God knows,' he said, tracing a finger down the sweet curve of her cheek with his thumb, 'you are that, but it is total nonsense. I did think of Rafe when I saw you that first day, because I know that he would have recognised what you were immediately.'

'And what is that?'

'My soul mate, the one woman I was destined to spend the rest of my life with. My brother always was more intuitive and much better with words than me.

'Me, I saw you standing there, the freckles on your nose, the hair like fire.' He sighed and looped a strand around his finger. 'I saw your belligerence, your bravery, your sheer bloody-minded stubbornness and I knew that I wanted to wake up every day looking at that face.'

The tears ran unchecked down Erin's cheeks. She was so happy she felt as though she might never walk at ground level again, but always float six inches above the ground.

'As for deceiving you—that was not deliberate, though I did perhaps seek to take advantage of your obvious affinity for cowboy boots.' He laughed when the colour flew to her cheeks. 'When we met I felt somehow that I was starting life afresh. I did not mention things because they did not seem important.'

By the time Francesco stopped talking there was a glazed look on Erin's face. 'I've been feeling so guilty—I felt as though I was taking advantage of you.'

'Because I was an emotional wreck,' he said drily. 'And now you know that I am not nearly so needy and vulnerable as you imagined, do you still want me?'

A rapturous smile spread across her face like the sun. 'I'll always want you.'

'Even if you learn that I will cheat, lie, manipulate and sell my soul in order to keep the one thing that I cannot live without.'

'If that one thing is me, I see no problem.'

The air left her lungs in one long gasp as he literally fell on her, his long body covering her as they sank down together on the sofa.

For some time they kissed and touched, passion flaring hot and out of control. It was Francesco who pulled away, rolling off her straight onto the floor where he lay on his back, breathing hard.

'What am I thinking? You just fainted and I jumped on you like a wild animal. The baby…!'

Erin, her face flushed, leaned over the side of the sofa and stroked his face. She was breathing hard.

'Wild?' she said, parting the front of his shirt with one fingertip—the buttons were scattered around the room—to reveal the red indentation where she had bitten into the smooth flesh of his shoulder.

She lifted an eloquent brow. 'As for baby,' she said, hand pressed to her tummy, 'I asked the doctor about that area and he said no restrictions there.'

'I know—I asked him, too.' He grinned as she dissolved into laughter.

She slipped from the sofa and sat astride him.

He lay there, one hand flung above his head, the other on the curve of her thigh. 'As much as I am enjoying being at your mercy, as you are the one who is meant to be recuperating should we not change places?'

'I am quite flexible.'

'This has not escaped my notice,' he growled throatily 'You know, this and the baby—I don't think life gets much better.'

'I can't believe we nearly got divorced.' She went pale at the thought.

'Getting your letter was a pretty big wake-up call for me.'

'So you would have come even if you hadn't found my phone and listened to the message?'

'I would have come. It was only ever my pride that was stopping me. I will not die if you leave me, but I will never be a whole man again. You,' he said, pressing his hand to his chest, 'are here. You complete me.'

Erin's eyes glowed with the love that lit her from within as she fell forward into his arms. She felt the sigh shudder through him as they closed tight around her.

She felt secure.

She felt safe.

She felt home.

She raised herself on her elbows and framed his proud, beautiful face in her hands. 'I will never, ever leave you, Francesco. How could I when I love you?'

When he pressed his mouth to hers she kissed him back offering all of herself to him with no restraints. When he dragged his mouth away they were both breathing hard.

She lifted a hand to her flame hair. 'God, I must look awful!'

The female vanity made Francesco grin. 'You look beautiful, but exhausted. I know you have an aversion to bedrest but I was wondering…?'

'How long did you have in mind?'

'Oh, a minimum two days…maybe three.'

She sighed. 'Well, if I *have* to.'

He ran a finger down the curve of her cheek. 'Sometimes I can't believe how beautiful you are.' He sighed, shaking his head at the wonder of having her. 'I came into the hospital that night just to watch you when you were asleep. I won't have to do that anymore—all I'll have to do is open my eyes because I warn you, Erin I've no intention of letting you out of my sight for a very long time. But right now we must obey the doctor.'

'Two days' bedrest?' She looped her arms happily around his neck.

'Minimum,' he confirmed.

'The bed part I think I could live with,' she said, looking at him with a naughty twinkle in her eyes. 'But I was wondering—does it have to be wall-to-wall rest? Can't I have time off for good behaviour?'

'Do you intend to be good?'

Erin, who had every intention of being quite bad, smiled into his eyes. He laughed. 'You're not going to be at all good, arc you?'

Erin fitted her mouth to her husband's and whispered against his lips, 'It wouldn't be me, would it?'

And the glorious thing was Francesco was the one man in the world she didn't have to pretend to be anyone else with.

Giving a contented sigh, she asked him if he had ever considered wearing his boots to bed.

His throaty burst of laughter rang out.

EPILOGUE

THERE was a gentle ripple of applause as the slim redhead walked into the room on the arm of a man with the looks of a dark fallen angel. She smiled and dipped her head in acknowledgement to the New York crowd.

'I think I'm dreaming,' she whispered to the man who walked beside her.

'No, *cara,* you're *living* the dream,' he told her. 'Go mingle—you're the star of this show.' For him she was the star of his life.

'Do I have to?'

He smiled encouragement. 'They'll love you, just smile and look enigmatic.'

The advice made her grin. 'You know what I'm afraid of?'

'What?'

'I'm afraid that someone is going to realise I'm a complete fake. I mean, why is this happening to me? I'm not special.'

'You're the most *special* person I have ever met, and, as for being a fake, I knew you were the real thing the moment I laid eyes on you. I just don't know how you do it,' he admitted.

'Do what?' she asked.

He was the best-looking man in the room by a mile and

after eighteen months of marriage Erin still looked at him sometimes and couldn't believe she had got that lucky.

'You're an incredible mother, you're an award-winning photographer, it's in no small part due to your efforts that my mother is her old self and, oh…I almost forgot—you're a fairly passable wife.'

Erin smiled back at him. 'What can I say? I'm brilliant!'

The past year and a bit had been incredible for her. Rafael was the most delicious baby in the world and looked just like his papa.

Rafael was a baby who seemed to bring out the best in people—even Erin's mother had been moved to tears when she'd first seen him, though she had not quite forgiven Erin for making her a granny. She wanted little Rafe to call her by her Christian name.

And she remained totally mystified by Erin's refusal to employ a personal trainer to get her figure back after the birth, hinting strongly that Francesco would look elsewhere unless she made an effort to compete with all those young lovelies with taut tummies.

But Erin's insecurities were well in the past and, secure in the knowledge that Francesco was totally devoted to her, Erin had been able to laugh at her mother's dire warnings. Besides, Francesco had expressed no complaints about any part of her anatomy. He had even found her sexy when she had been the size of a small supermarket…which was odd, but nice.

Rafe's other grandma was not concerned about her daughter-in-law's waistline—in her eyes giving birth to little Rafe had elevated Erin's status to a level where she was above criticism. She adored her little grandson and had come with them to New York so that she could look after him while Francesco and Erin attended the opening night of Erin's new exhibition.

After some heated discussion on the subject Francesco had reluctantly conceded on the subject of a nanny. And when he had seen that, far from being exhausted—beyond what was normal—by the task of bringing up baby the new mother had thrived he had stopped worrying.

Of course, in the future she might rethink the nanny ban because in about seven months' time Rafael would have some company.

The news that she was carrying twins was still sinking in!

Francesco was still inclined to stop dead in the middle of the street without warning and say, '*Twins!*' Which made people stare at him.

After her labour with Rafael he had declared that his son was *definitely* going to be an only child because he could not go through that ever again!

Erin still had seven months to convince him that to try for a normal birth with twins was not really quite as recklessly stupid as he contended.

The London exhibition the previous year had been a massive success and it had kick started her new career. She now had her photos hanging in galleries and private collections all over Europe and after tonight who knew? Maybe the States, too...

But no matter how her career went for Erin, her family was the most important thing in her life. And within that tight circle it was Francesco who made her believe she could succeed, he enhanced every aspect of her life just because he was there.

Francesco bent his head and whispered in his wife's ear. 'How do you always make my heart beat faster?'

Her breath caught in her throat at the tenderness in his eyes.

'I love you so much!' she whispered. 'In fact,' she confided happily, 'my cup pretty much runneth over. I'm so happy I might explode any minute.'

'The exploding might have more to do with the twins,' Francesco suggested drily.

'Gosh, is that the scary critic?' she asked, watching a small balding man with an air of vast self-importance approach.

'That is Felix Mortimer himself,' Francesco confirmed. 'He's smiling—you have made it, *cara*. I can see that I will have to get used to myself referred to as Erin Romanelli's husband.'

Erin lifted her head for his kiss. 'I love you so much.'

'And I love you, but now run along—your public await.' He tapped her encouragingly on the bottom.

He watched with pride as she was greeted obsequiously by the critic. Francesco smiled. He could spare his Erin for a little while, because Francesco knew that she would always come back to him.

THE ROYAL HOUSE OF NIROLI

...International affairs, seduction and passion guaranteed

Volume 1 – July 2007
The Future King's Pregnant Mistress by Penny Jordan

Volume 2 – August 2007
Surgeon Prince, Ordinary Wife by Melanie Milburne

Volume 3 – September 2007
Bought by the Billionaire Prince by Carol Marinelli

Volume 4 – October 2007
The Tycoon's Princess Bride by Natasha Oakley

8 volumes in all to collect!

THE ROYAL HOUSE OF NIROLI

...International affairs, seduction and passion guaranteed

VOLUME TWO

Surgeon Prince, Ordinary Wife
by Melanie Milburne

His first heir excluded from the throne, the King summons his family to his side... Then discovers the grandson he thought was dead is still very much alive!

Alessandro Fierezza was snatched as a baby and held for ransom by ruthless Vialli bandits. But when brilliant Australian surgeon Dr Alex Hunter arrives on Niroli to help the ailing king, rumours abound that he is the missing prince!

Amelia Vialli is a dedicated nurse, helping the poor of Niroli, but has had to live with the stigma of being a Vialli bandit all her life. When Dr Hunter appears, Amelia falls instantly under his spell, unaware of the intrigue that surrounds him.

But when Alex discovers the truth, he's torn between duty to the ruling family he's never known and his passion for an ordinary woman who can never be his queen...

Available 3rd August 2007

www.millsandboon.co.uk

M&B

4 FREE

BOOKS AND A SURPRISE GIFT!

We would like to take this opportunity to thank you for reading this Mills & Boon® book by offering you the chance to take FOUR more specially selected titles from the Modern™ series absolutely FREE! We're also making this offer to introduce you to the benefits of the Mills & Boon® Reader Service™—

- ★ FREE home delivery
- ★ FREE gifts and competitions
- ★ FREE monthly Newsletter
- ★ Exclusive Reader Service offers
- ★ Books available before they're in the shops

Accepting these FREE books and gift places you under no obligation to buy, you may cancel at any time, even after receiving your free shipment. Simply complete your details below and return the entire page to the address below. You don't even need a stamp!

YES! Please send me 4 free Modern books and a surprise gift. I understand that unless you hear from me, I will receive 6 superb new titles every month for just £2.89 each, postage and packing free. I am under no obligation to purchase any books and may cancel my subscription at any time. The free books and gift will be mine to keep in any case.

P7ZED

Ms/Mrs/Miss/Mr ....Initials ....
BLOCK CAPITALS PLEASE

Surname ....

Address ....

....

....Postcode..........................

Send this whole page to:
UK: FREEPOST CN81, Croydon, CR9 3WZ